Story of Aeneas

Michael Clarke

Alpha Editions

This edition published in 2024

ISBN : 9789362926784

Design and Setting By
Alpha Editions
www.alphaedis.com
Email - info@alphaedis.com

As per information held with us this book is in Public Domain.
This book is a reproduction of an important historical work. Alpha Editions uses the best technology to reproduce historical work in the same manner it was first published to preserve its original nature. Any marks or number seen are left intentionally to preserve its true form.

Contents

INTRODUCTION. ....- 1 -

I. THE WOODEN HORSE, ...- 6 -

II. AENEAS LEAVES TROY—THE
HARPIES—PROPHECY OF HELENUS-
THE GIANT POLYPHEMUS. ....- 14 -

III. A GREAT STORM—ARRIVAL IN
CARTHAGE. ....- 21 -

IV. DIDO'S LOVE—THE FUNERAL
GAMES—SHIPS BURNED BY THE
WOMEN. ....- 29 -

V. THE SIBYL OF CUMAE—THE
GOLDEN BOUGH—IN THE REGIONS
OF THE DEAD. ....- 38 -

VI. AENEAS ARRIVES IN LATIUM—
WELCOMED BY KING LATINUS. ....- 46 -

VII. ALLIANCE WITH EVANDER—
VULCAN MAKES ARMS FOR
AENEAS—THE FAMOUS SHIELD. ....- 56 -

VIII. TURNUS ATTACKS THE TROJAN
CAMP—NISUS AND EURYALUS. ....- 65 -

IX. THE COUNCIL OF THE GODS—
RETURN OF AENEAS—BATTLE ON
THE SHORE— DEATH OF PALLAS. ....- 74 -

X. FUNERAL OF PALLAS—AENEAS AND TURNUS FIGHT—TURNUS IS SLAIN. ....- 81 -

INTRODUCTION.

I. VERGIL, THE PRINCE OF LATIN POETS.

The story of AE-ne'as, as related by the Roman poet Ver'gil in his celebrated poem called the AE-ne'id, which we are to tell about in this book, is one of the most interesting of the myths or legends that have come down to us from ancient authors.

Vergil lived in the time of the Roman Emperor Au-gus'tus (63 B. C.—14 A. D.), grand-nephew and successor of Ju'li-us Cae'sar. Augustus and his chief counsellor or minister Mae-ce'nas, gave great encouragement to learning and learned men, and under their liberal patronage arose a number of eminent writers to whose works has been given the name of classics, as being of the highest rank or *class*. The period is known as the Augustan Age, a phrase also used in reference to periods in the history of other countries, in which literature reached its highest perfection. Thus the reign of Queen Anne (1702-1714) is called the Augustan age of English literature, because of the number of literary men who flourished in England in that period, and the excellence of their works.

Vergil was the greatest of the poets of ancient Rome, and with the exception of Ho'mer, the greatest of the poets of antiquity. From a very early period, almost from the age in which he lived, he was called the Prince of Latin Poets. His full name was Pub'li-us Ver-gil'i-us Ma'ro. He was born about seventy years before Christ, in the village of An'des (now Pi-e'to-le), near the town of Man'tu-a in the north of Italy. His father was the owner of a small estate, which he farmed himself. Though of moderate means, he gave his son a good education. Young Vergil spent his boyhood at school at Cre-mo'na and Milan. He completed his studies at Naples, where he read the Greek and Latin authors, and acquired a knowledge of mathematics, natural philosophy, and medical science. He afterwards returned to Mantua, and resided there for a few years, enjoying the quiet of country life at the family homestead.

About this time the Emperor Augustus was engaged in a war against a powerful party of his own countrymen, led by a famous Roman named Bru'tus. In the year 42 B.C. he defeated Brutus in a great battle, which put an end to the war. He afterwards rewarded many of his troops by dividing among them lands in the neighborhood of Mantua, and in other parts of Italy, dispossessing the owners for having sided with his enemies. Though Vergil had taken no part in the struggle, his farm was allotted to one of the imperial soldiers. But this was the beginning of his greatness. Through the friendship of the governor of Mantua, he was introduced to Maecenas, and afterwards to Augustus, who gave orders that his property should be restored to him.

Thus Vergil became known to the first men of Rome. He expressed his gratitude to the emperor in one of a series of poems called Pastorals or Bu-col'ics, words which mean shepherds' songs, or songs descriptive of life in the country. These poems, though among Vergil's earliest productions, were highly applauded in Rome. They were so much esteemed that portions of them were recited in the theatre in the author's presence, and the audience were so delighted that they all rose to their feet, an honor which it was customary to pay only to Augustus himself. Vergil also wrote a poem called the Geor'gics, the subject of which is agriculture, the breeding of cattle, and the culture of bees. This is said to be the most perfect in finish of all Latin compositions. The AEneid is, however, regarded as the greatest of Vergil's works. The writing of it occupied the last eleven years of the poet's life.

Vergil died at Brun-di'si-um, in south Italy, in the fifty-first year of his age. He was buried near Naples, by the side of the public road, a few miles outside that city, where what is said to be his tomb is still to be seen. Of his character as a man we are enabled to form an agreeable idea from all that is known about him. He was modest, gentle and of a remarkable sweetness of disposition. Although living in the highest society while in Rome, he never forgot his old friends. He was a dutiful and affectionate son, and liberally shared his good fortune with his aged parents.

As a poet, Vergil was not only the greatest that Rome produced, but the most popular. His poems, particularly the AEneid, were the favorite reading of his countrymen. They became a text-book in the Roman schools. The "little Romans," we are told, studied the AEneid from their master's dictation, and wrote compositions upon its heroes. And not alone in Italy but throughout the world wherever learning extended, the AEneid became popular, and has retained its popularity down to our own time, being still a text-book in every school where Latin is taught.

There are many excellent translations of the AEneid into English. In this book we make numerous quotations from the translation by the English poet Dryden, and from the later work by the eminent Latin scholar Conington.

SPELLING OF THE POET'S NAME.

The spelling of the poet's name adopted in this book is now believed to be preferable to the form V_i_rgil which has for a long time been in common use. Many of the best Latin scholars are of opinion that the proper spelling is V_e_rgil from the Latin V_e_rgilius, as the poet himself wrote it. "As to the fact," says Professor Frieze, "that the poet called himself Vergilius, scholars are now universally agreed. It is the form found in all the earliest manuscripts and inscriptions. In England and America the corrected Latin form is used by all the best authorities."

II. THE GODS AND GODDESSES.

It is said that Vergil wrote the AEneid at the request of the Emperor Augustus, whose family—the Ju'li-i—claimed the honor of being descended from AEneas, through his son I-u'lus or Ju'lus. All the Romans, indeed, were fond of claiming descent from the heroes whom tradition told of as having landed in Italy with AEneas after escaping from the ruins of Troy. The city of Troy, or Il'i-um, so celebrated in ancient song and story, was situated on the coast of Asia Minor, not far from the entrance to what is now the Sea of Mar'mo-ra. It was besieged for ten years by a vast army of the Greeks (natives of Greece or Hel'las) under one of their kings called Ag-a-mem'non. Homer, the greatest of the ancient poets, tells about this siege in his famous poem, the Il'i-ad. We shall see later on how the siege was brought to an end by the capture and destruction of the city, as well as how AEneas escaped, and what afterwards happened to him and his companions.

Meanwhile we must learn something about the gods and goddesses who play so important a part in the story. At almost every stage of the adventures of AEneas, as of the adventures of all ancient heroes, we find a god or a goddess controlling or directing affairs, or in some way mixed up with the course of events.

According to the religion of the ancient Greeks and Romans there were a great many gods. They believed that all parts of the universe—the heavens and the earth, the sun and the moon, the seas and rivers, and storms—were ruled by different gods. Those beings it was supposed, were in some respects like men and women. They needed food and drink and sleep; they married and had children; and like poor mortals they often had quarrels among themselves. Their food was am-bro'si-a, which gave them immortality and perpetual youth, and their drink was a delicious wine called nectar.

The gods often visited men and even accepted their hospitality. Sometimes they married human beings, and the sons of such marriages were the demigods or heroes of antiquity. AEneas was one of those heroes, his mother being the goddess Ve'nus, of whom we shall hear much in the course of our Story.

Though the gods never died, being immortal, they might be wounded and suffer bodily pain like men. They often took part in the quarrels and wars of people on earth, and they had weapons and armor, after the manner of earthly warriors. But they were vastly superior to men in strength and power. They could travel through the skies, or upon land or ocean, with the speed of lightning, and they could change themselves into any form, or make themselves visible or invisible at pleasure.

The usual residence of the principal gods was on the top of Mount O-lym'pus, in Greece. Here they had golden palaces and a chamber where they held grand banquets at which celestial music was rendered by A-pol'lo, the god of minstrelsy, and the Muses, who were the divinities of poetry and song.

Splendid temples were erected to the gods in all the chief cities, where they were worshiped with many ceremonies. Valuable gifts in gold and silver were presented at their shrines, and at their altars animals were killed and portions of the flesh burned as sacrifices. Such offerings were thought to be very pleasing to the gods.

The head or king of the gods was Ju'pi-ter, also called Jove or Zeus. He was the great Thunderer, at whose word the heavens trembled.

> He, whose all conscious eyes the world behold,
> The eternal Thunderer sat enthroned in gold.
> High heaven the footstool of his feet he makes,
> And wide beneath him all Olympus shakes.
> HOMER, *Iliad*, BOOK VIII.

The wife of Jupiter, and the queen of heaven, was Ju'no, who, as we shall see, persecuted the hero AEneas with "unrelenting hate." Nep'tune, represented as bearing in his hand a trident, or three- pronged fork, was the god of the sea.

> Neptune, the mighty marine god,
> Earth's mover, and the fruitless ocean's king.
> HOMER

Mars was the god of war, and Plu'to, often called Dis or Ha'des, was the god of the lower or "infernal" regions, and hence also the god of the dead. One of the most glorious and beautiful of the gods was Apollo, god of the sun, of medicine, music, poetry, and all fine arts.

> Bright-hair'd Apollo!—thou who ever art
> A blessing to the world—whose mighty heart
> Forever pours out love, and light, and life;
> Thou, at whose glance, all things of earth are rife

With happiness.
                    PIKE.

[Illustration: A ROMAN AUGUR.]

Another of the famous divinities of the ancients was Venus, the goddess of beauty and love. According to some of the myths she was the daughter of Jupiter. Others say that she sprang from the foam of the sea.

These and countless other imaginary beings were believed in as deities under the religious system of the ancient Greeks and Romans, and every unusual or striking event was thought to be caused by some god or goddess.

The will of the gods, it was supposed, was made known to men in different ways—by dreams, by the flight of birds, or by a direct message from Olympus. Very often it was learned by consulting seers, augurs or soothsayers. These were persons believed to have the power of prophecy. There was a famous temple of Apollo at Delphi, in Greece, where a priestess called Pyth'i-a gave answers, or oracles, to those who came to consult her. The name oracle was also applied to the place where such answers were received. There were a great many oracles in ancient times, but that at Delphi was the most celebrated.

I. THE WOODEN HORSE,

The gods, of course, had much to do with the siege and fall of Troy, as well as with the sufferings of Aeneas, which Vergil describes in the AEneid. There were gods and goddesses on both sides in the great conflict. Some were for the Tro'jans, others for the Greeks, and some had their favorites among the heroes and warriors who fought on one side or the other. Two very powerful goddesses, Juno and Mi-ner'va (the goddess of wisdom, also called Pallas), hated the Trojans because of the famous "judgment of Pa'ris," which came about in this way—.

A king of Athens named Pe'leus married a beautiful sea-nymph named The'tis. All the gods and goddesses were present at the wedding feast except E'ris, the goddess of discord. She was not invited, and being angry on that account, she resolved to cause dissension among the guests. With this object she threw into the midst of the assembly a golden apple bearing the inscription, "For the most beautiful." Immediately a dispute arose as to which of the goddesses was entitled to the prize, but at last all gave up their claim except Juno, Venus, and Minerva, and they agreed to leave the settlement of the question to Paris, son of Pri'am, King of Troy, a young prince who was noted for the wisdom of his judgments upon several occasions.

The three goddesses soon afterwards appeared before Paris, and each endeavored by the offer of tempting bribes, to induce him to decide in her favor. Juno promised him great power and wealth.

> She to Paris made
> Proffer of royal power, ample rule
> Unquestion'd.
>
> TENNYSON.

Minerva offered military glory, and Venus promised that she would give him the most beautiful woman in the world for his wife. After hearing their claims and promises, Paris gave the apple to Venus. This award or judgment brought upon him and his family, and all the Trojans, the hatred of the two other goddesses, particularly of Juno, who, being the queen of heaven, had expected that the preference, as a matter of course would be given to her.

But besides the judgment of Paris, there was another cause of Juno's anger against Troy. She had heard of a decree of the Fates that a race descended from the Trojans was one day to destroy Carthage, a city in which she was worshipped with much honor, and which she regarded with great affection.

She therefore hated Aeneas, through whom, as the ancestor of the founders of Rome, the destruction of her beloved city was to be brought about.

On account of this hatred of the Trojans, Juno persuaded her royal husband, Jupiter, to consent to the downfall of Troy, and so the valor of all its heroic defenders, of whom Aeneas was one, could not save it from its fate, decreed by the king of the gods. Many famous warriors fell during the long siege. Hec'tor, son of Priam, the greatest of the Trojan champions, was slain by A-chil'les, the most valiant of the Greeks, and Achilles was himself slain by Paris. After losing their bravest leader the Greeks despaired of being able to take the city by force, and so they resorted to stratagem. By the advice of Minerva they erected a huge horse of wood on the plain in front of the walls, and within its body they placed a chosen band of their boldest warriors. Then pretending that they had given up the struggle, they withdrew to their ships, and set sail, as if with the purpose of returning to Greece. But they went no further than Ten'e-dos, an island opposite Troy, a few miles from the coast.

> "There was their fleet concealed. We thought for Greece
> Their sails were hoisted, and our fears release.
> The Trojans, cooped within their walls so long,
> Unbar their gates and issue in a throng
> Like swarming bees, and with delight survey
> The camp deserted, where the Grecians lay:
> The quarters of the several chiefs they showed:
> Here Phoe'nix, here Achilles, made abode;
> Here joined the battles; there the navy rode.
> Part on the pile their wandering eyes employ—
> The pile by Pallas raised to ruin Troy."
>   DRYDEN, *AEneid*, BOOK II.

The Trojans when they saw the big horse, could not think what it meant, or what should be done with it. Various opinions were given. Some thought it was a peace offering, and one chief proposed that it should be dragged within the walls and placed in the citadel. Others advised that it should be cast into the sea, or set on fire, or at least that they ought to burst it open to find whether anything were concealed within. While they were thus discussing the matter, some urging one course, some another, the priest La-oc'o-on rushed out from the city followed by a great crowd and he exclaimed in a loud voice: "Unhappy fellow-countrymen, what madness is this? Are you so foolish as to suppose that the enemy are gone, or that any offering of theirs can be free from deception? Either Greeks are hidden in this horse, or it is an engine designed for some evil to our city. Put no faith in it, Trojans. Whatever it is, I fear the Greeks even when they tender gifts." Thus speaking, Laocoon hurled his spear into the horse's side.

> His mighty spear he cast:
> Quivering it stood: the sharp rebound
> Shook the huge monster: and a sound
> Through all its caverns passed.
>   CONINGTON, *AEneid*, BOOK II.

But at this point the attention of the multitude was attracted by the appearance of a group of Trojan shepherds dragging along a prisoner with his hands bound behind his back, who, they said, had delivered himself up to them of his own accord. Being taken before King Priam, and questioned as to who he was and whence he came, the stranger told an artful story. He was a Greek, he said, and his name was Si'non. His countrymen had long been weary of the war, and had often resolved to return home, but were hindered by storms from making the attempt. And when the wooden horse was built, the tempests raged and the thunder rolled more than ever.

> "Chiefly when completed stood
> This horse, compact of maple wood,
> Fierce thunders, pealing in our ears,
> Proclaimed the turmoil of the spheres."
>   CONINGTON, *AEneid*, BOOK II.

Then the Greeks sent a messenger to the shrine of Apollo to inquire how they might obtain a safe passage to their country. The answer was that the life of a Greek must be sacrificed on the altar of the god. All were horror-stricken by this announcement, for each feared that the doom might fall upon himself.

> "Through every heart a shudder ran,
> 'Apollo's victim—who the man?'"
>   CONINGTON, *AEneid*, BOOK II.

The selection of the person to be the victim was left to Cal'chas, the soothsayer, who fixed upon Sinon, and preparations were accordingly made to sacrifice him on the altar of Apollo, but he contrived to escape and conceal himself until the Grecian fleet had sailed.

> "I fled, I own it, from the knife,
> I broke my bands and ran for life,
> And in a marsh lay that night
> While they should sail, if sail they might."
>   CONINGTON, *AEneid*, BOOK II.

This was Sinon's story. The Trojans believed it and King Priam ordered the prisoner to be released, and promised to give him protection in Troy. "But tell me," said the king, "why did they make this horse? Was it for a religious purpose or as an engine of war?" The treacherous Sinon answered that the horse was intended as a peace offering to the gods; that it had been built on the advice of Calchas, who had directed that it should be made of immense size so that the Trojans should not be able to drag it within their walls, "for," said he, "if the men of Troy do any injury to the gift, evil will come upon the kingdom of Priam, but if they bring it into their city, all Asia will make war against Greece, arid on our children will come the destruction which we would have brought upon Troy."

The Trojans believed this story also, and their belief was strengthened by the terrible fate which just then befell Laocoon, who a little before had pierced the side of the horse with his spear. While the priest and his two sons were offering a sacrifice to Neptune on the shore, two enormous serpents suddenly issued from the sea and seized and crushed them to death in sight of the people. The Trojans were filled with fear and astonishment at this spectacle, and they regarded the event as a punishment from the gods upon Laocoon.

> Who dared to harm with impious steel
> Those planks of consecrated deal.
> CONINGTON, *AEneid*, BOOK II.

Then a cry arose that the "peace offering" should be conveyed into the city, and accordingly a great breach was made in the walls that for ten years had resisted all the assaults of the Greeks, and by means of rollers attached to its feet, and ropes tied around its limbs, the horse was dragged into the citadel, the young men and maidens singing songs of triumph. But in the midst of the rejoicing there were portents of the approaching evil. Four times the huge figure halted on the threshold of the gate, and four times it gave forth a sound from within, as if of the clash of arms.

> "Four times 'twas on the threshold stayed:
> Four times the armor clashed and brayed.
> Yet on we press with passion blind,
> All forethought blotted from our mind,
> Till the dread monster we install
> Within the temple's tower-built wall."
> CONINGTON. *AEneid*, BOOK II.

The prophetess Cas-san'dra, too, the daughter of King Priam, had warned her countrymen of the doom that was certain to fall upon the city if the horse were admitted. Her warning was, however, disregarded. The fateful gift of the Greeks was placed in the citadel, and the Trojans, thinking that their troubles were now over, and that the enemy had departed to return no more, spent the rest of the day in feasting and rejoicing.

But in the dead of the night, when they were all sunk in sleep, the Greek fleet sailed back from Tenedos, and on King Agamemnon's ship a bright light was shown, which was the signal to the false Sinon to complete his work of treachery. Quickly he "unlocked the horse" and forth from their hiding place came the armed Greek warriors. Among them were the famous U-lys'ses, and Ne-op-tol'e-mus, son of the brave Achilles, and Men-e-la'us, husband of the celebrated Hel'en whom Paris, son of Priam, had carried off from Greece, which was the cause of the war. Ulysses and his companions then rushed to the walls, and after slaying the sentinels, threw open the gates of the city to the main body of the Greeks who had by this time landed from their ships. Thus Troy was taken.

> And the long baffled legions, bursting in
> Through gate and bastion, blunted sword and spear
> With unresisted slaughter.
> LEWIS MORRIS.

Meanwhile AEneas, sleeping in the house of his father, An-chi'ses, had a dream in which the ghost of Hector appeared to him, shedding abundant tears, and disfigured with wounds as when he had been dragged around the walls of Troy behind the chariot of the victorious Achilles. In a mournful voice, AEneas, seeming to forget that Hector was dead, inquired why he had been so long absent from the defense of his native city, and from what distant shores he had now returned. But the spirit answered only by a solemn warning to AEneas, the "goddess- born" (being the son of Venus) to save himself by immediate flight.

> "O goddess-born! escape by timely flight,
> The flames and horrors of this fatal night.
> The foes already have possessed the wall;
> Troy nods from high, and totters to her fall.
> Enough is paid to Priam's royal name,
> More than enough to duty and to fame.
> If by a mortal hand my father's throne
> Could be defended, 'twas by mine alone.
> Now Troy to thee commends her future state,
> And gives her gods companions of thy fate;
> From their assistance, happier walls expect,
> Which, wand'ring long, at last thou shalt erect."
> DRYDEN, *AEneid*, BOOK I.

Awaking from his sleep, AEneas was startled by the clash of arms and by cries of battle, which he now heard on all sides. Rushing to the roof of the house and gazing around, he saw the palaces of many of the Trojan princes in flames, and he heard the shouts of the victorious Greeks, and the blaring of their trumpets. Notwithstanding the warning of Hector, he ran for his weapons.

> Resolved on death, resolved to die in arms,
> But first to gather friends, with them to oppose
> (If fortune favored) and repel the foes.
> DRYDEN, *AEneid*, BOOK II.

At the door, as he was going forth to join the combat, he met the Trojan Pan'thus, a priest of Apollo, who had just escaped by flight from the swords of the Greeks. In reply to the questions of AEneas, the priest told him, in words of grief and despair, that Troy's last day had come.

> "'Tis come, our fated day of death.
> We have been Trojans; Troy has been;
> She sat, but sits no more, a queen;
> Stern Jove an Argive rule proclaims;
> Greece holds a city wrapt in flames.
> There in the bosom of the town
> The tall horse rains invasion down,
> And Sinon, with a conqueror's pride,
> Deals fiery havoc far and wide.
> Some keep the gates, as vast a host
> As ever left Myce'nae's coast;
> Some block the narrows of the street,
> With weapons threatening all they meet;
> The stark sword stretches o'er the way,
> Quick-glancing, ready drawn to slay,
> While scarce our sentinels resist,
> And battle in the flickering mist."
> CONINGTON, *AEneid*, BOOK II.

As Panthus ceased speaking, several Trojan chiefs came up, and eagerly joined AEneas in resolving to make a last desperate attempt to save their native city. Together they rushed into the thick of the fight. Some were slain, and some with Aeneas succeeded in forcing their way to the palace of King Priam, where a fierce struggle was then raging. Entering by a secret door, AEneas climbed to the roof, from which he and the other brave defenders of the palace hurled stones and beams of wood upon the enemy below. But all their heroic efforts were in vain. In front of the principal gate, battering upon it with his huge battle-axe, stood Neoptolemus (also called Pyr'rhus) the son of Achilles. Soon its posts, though plated with bronze, gave way before his mighty strokes, and a great breach was made, through which the Greeks poured into the stately halls of the Trojan king. Then there was a scene of wild confusion and terror.

> The house is filled with loud laments and cries
> And shrieks of women rend the vaulted skies.
>   DRYDEN, *AEneid* BOOK II.

The aged king when he saw that the enemy was beneath his roof, put on his armor "long disused," and was about to rush forth to meet the foe, but Hec'u-ba, his queen, persuaded him to take refuge with her in a court of the palace in which were placed the altars of their gods. Here he was shortly afterwards cruelly slain by Pyrrhus.

> Thus Priam fell, and shared one common fate
> With Troy in ashes, and his ruined state;
> He, who the scepter of all Asia swayed,
> Whom monarchs like domestic slaves obeyed.
>   DRYDEN, *AEneid*, BOOK II.

There being now no hope to save the city, the thoughts of AEneas turned to his own home where he had left his father Anchises, his wife Cre-u'sa (daughter of King Priam) and his son Iulus (also named As-ca'ni-us). Making his way thither with the purpose of providing for their safety, he espied Helen, the "common scourge of Greece and Troy," sitting in the porch of the temple of the goddess Ves'ta. Enraged at the sight of the woman who had been the cause of so many woes to his country, AEneas was about to slay her on the spot, but at that moment his mother Venus appeared to him in the midst of a bright light.

> Great in her charms, as when on gods above
> She looks, and breathes herself into their love.
>   DRYDEN, *AEneid*, BOOK II.

Taking the hero by the hand as he was in the act of raising his sword to strike Helen, the goddess thus rebuked him: "What is it that excites your anger now, my son? Where is your regard for me? Have you forgotten your father Anchises and your wife and little son? They would have been killed by the Greeks if I had not cared for them and saved them. It is not Helen or Paris that has laid low this great city of Troy, but the wrath of the gods. See now, for I will take away the mist that covers your mortal eyes; see how Neptune with his trident is overthrowing the walls and rooting up the city from its foundations; and how Juno stands with spear and shield in the Scae'an Gate, and calls fresh hosts from the ships; and how Pallas sits on the height with the storm-cloud about her; and how Father Jupiter himself stirs up the enemy against Troy. Fly, therefore, my son. I myself will guard you till you stand before your father's door."

The goddess then disappeared and AEneas quickly proceeded to obey her command. Hastening home he resolved to take his aged father to a place of safety in the hills beyond the city, but the old man refused to go. "You, who are young and strong," said he, "may go, but I shall remain here, for if it had been the will of the gods that I should live, they would have preserved my home."

"Now leave me: be your farewell said
To this my corpse, and count me dead."
CONINGTON, *AEneid*, BOOK II

Nor could all the entreaties of his son and wife move him from his resolution. Then AEneas, in grief and despair, was about to rush back to the battle, which still raged in the city, preferring to die rather than to go and leave his father behind. But at this moment a bright flame as if of fire was seen to play around the head of the boy Iulus, and send forth beams of light. Alarmed as well as surprised at the spectacle, AEneas was about to extinguish the flames by water, when Anchises cried out that it was a sign from heaven that he should accompany his family in their flight from the city.

This pretty story, it is said, was meant by Vergil as a compliment to Augustus, the idea intended to be conveyed being that the seal of sovereign power was thus early set upon the founder of the great house of Julius.

[Illustration: AEneas carrying his father out of Troy. (Drawn by Varian.)]

The gods seeming thus to ordain the immediate departure of the hero and his family, they all speedily set forth, AEneas carrying his father on his shoulders, while Iulus walked by his side, and Creusa followed at some distance. They had arranged to meet at a ruined temple outside the city, where they were to be joined by their servants, but when they reached the place, it was discovered that Creusa had disappeared. Great was the grief of Aeneas. In agony he hastened back to the city in search of his wife. Coming to his father's palace, he found it already in flames. Then he hurried on through the streets, in his distress calling aloud the name of Creusa. Suddenly her figure started up before him, larger than when in life, for it was her spirit he saw. Appalled at the sight, Aeneas stood in silence gazing at the apparition while it thus spoke:

"Beloved husband, why do you give way to grief? What has happened is by the decree of heaven. It was not the will of the gods that I should accompany you. You have a long journey to make, and a wide extent of sea to cross, before you reach the shores of Hes-pe'ri-a, where the Ti'ber flows in gentle course through the rich fields of a warlike race. There prosperity awaits you, and you shall take to yourself a wife of a royal line. Weep not for me. The mother of the gods keeps me in this land to serve her. And now farewell, and fail not to love and watch over our son."

Then the form of Creusa melted into air, and the sorrowing husband returned to the place where his father and son awaited him. There he found a number of his fellow-citizens prepared to follow him into exile. They first took refuge in the forests of Mount I'da, not far from the ruined city. In this place they spent the winter, and they built a fleet of ships at Antan'dros, a coast town at the foot of the mountain.

> "Near old Antandros, and at Ida's foot,
> The timber of the sacred groves we cut,
> And build our fleet-uncertain yet to find
> What place the gods for our repose assigned."
> DRYDEN, *AEneid*, BOOK III.

It is remarkable that Vergil does not tell how Creusa came by her death. Apparently we are left to infer that she was killed by the Greeks.

II. AENEAS LEAVES TROY—THE HARPIES—PROPHECY OF HELENUS-THE GIANT POLYPHEMUS.

In the early days of summer—the fleet being ready and all preparations complete—Anchises gave the order for departure, and so they set sail, piously carrying with them the images of their household gods and of the "great gods" of their nation. The first land they touched was the coast of Thrace, not far from Troy. AEneas thought he would build a city and make a settlement here, as the country had been, from early times, connected by ties of friendship with his own. To obtain the blessing of heaven on an undertaking of such importance, he set about performing religious services in honor of his mother Venus and the other gods, sacrificing a snow-white bull as an offering to Jupiter. Close by the place there happened to be a little hill, on the top of which was a grove of myrtle, bristling with thick-clustering, spear-like shoots. Wishing to have some of those plants to decorate his altars, AEneas pulled one up from the ground, whereupon he beheld drops of blood oozing from the torn roots. Though horrified at the sight he plucked another bough, and again blood oozed out as before. Then praying to the gods to save himself and his people from whatever evil there might be in the omen, he proceeded to tear up a third shoot, when from out the earth at his feet a voice uttered these words:

"O, AEneas! why do you tear an unhappy wretch? Spare me, now that I am in my grave; forbear to pollute your pious hands. It is from no tree-trunk that the blood comes. Quit this barbarous land with all speed. Know that I am Pol-y-do'rus. Here I was slain by many arrows, which have taken root and grown into a tree."

Deep was the horror of AEneas while he listened to this dreadful story, for he knew that Polydorus was one of the younger sons of Priam. Early in the war, his father, fearing that the Trojans might be defeated, had sent him for protection to the court of the king of Thrace. At the same time he sent the greater part of his treasures, including a large sum of money, to be taken care of by the king till the war should be over. But as soon as the Thracian monarch heard of the fall of Troy he treacherously slew the young prince and seized all his father's treasure.

> False to divine and human laws,
> The traitor joins the conqueror's cause,
> Lays impious hands on Polydore,
> And grasps by force the golden store.
> Fell lust of gold! abhorred, accurst!
> What will not men to slake such thirst?
> CONINGTON, *AEneid*, BOOK III.

When AEneas related this story to his father and the other Trojan chiefs, they all agreed to depart forthwith from a land polluted by so black a crime. But first they performed funeral rites on the grave of Polydorus, erecting two altars which they decked with cypress wreaths, the emblem of mourning, and offering sacrifices to the gods.

Soon afterwards, the winds being favorable, they set sail, and in a few days reached De'los, one of the isles of Greece, where there was a famous temple of Apollo. A'ni-us, the king of the island, and a priest of Apollo, gave them a hospitable reception. In the great temple they made suitable offerings, and AEneas prayed to the god to tell them in what country they might find a resting place and a home. Scarcely had the prayer been finished when the temple and the earth itself seemed to quake, whereupon the Trojans prostrated themselves in lowly reverence upon the ground, and presently they heard a voice saying: "Brave sons of Dar'da-nus, the land which gave birth to your ancestors shall again receive your race in its fertile bosom. Seek out your ancient mother. There the house of AEneas shall rule over every coast, and his children's children and their descendants."

The answers or oracles of the gods were often given in mysterious words, as in the present case. AEneas and his companions did not know what land was meant by the "ancient mother," but Anchises, "revolving in his mind the legends of the men of old," remembered having heard that one of his ancestors, Teu'cer, (the father-in-law of Dardanus), had come from the island of Crete. Believing, therefore, that that was the land referred to in the words of the oracle, they set sail, having first sacrificed to Apollo, to Neptune, god of the ocean, and to the god of storms, that their voyage might be favorable.

> A bull to Neptune, an oblation due,
> Another bull to bright Apollo slew;
> A milk-white ewe, the western winds to please
> And one coal-black, to calm the stormy seas.
>   DRYDEN, *AEneid*, BOOK III.

They arrived safely at Crete (now known as Can'di-a) where they remained a considerable time and built a city which AEneas called Per'ga-mus, the name of the famous citadel or fort of Troy. But here a new misfortune came upon the exiles in the shape of a plague, which threatened destruction to man and beast and the fruits of the field.

> Sudden on man's feeble frame
> From tainted skies a sickness came,
> On trees and crops a poisonous breath,
> A year of pestilence and death.
>   CONINGTON, *AEneid*, BOOK III.

Anchises now proposed that they should return to Delos, and again seek the counsel and aid of Apollo, but that night AEneas had a dream in which the household gods whose images he had carried with him from Troy, appeared to him, and told him that Crete was not the land destined by the gods for him and his people. They also told him where that Hesperia was, of which he had heard from the shade of Creusa.

> "A land there is, Hesperia called of old,
> (The soil is fruitful, and the natives bold—
> The OE-no'tri-ans held it once,) by later fame
> Now called I-ta'li-a, from the leader's name.
> I-a'si-us there, and Dardanus, were born:
> From thence we came, and thither must return.
> Rise, and thy sire with these glad tidings greet:
> Search Italy: for Jove denies thee Crete."
>   DRYDEN, *AEneid*, BOOK III.

AEneas made haste to tell this dream to his father, whereupon the old man advised that they should at once depart. So they quickly got their ships in order and set sail for Hesperia—the Land of the West. But scarcely had they lost sight of the shore when a terrible storm arose which drove them out of their course, and for three days and nights the light of heaven was shut from their view. Even the great Pal-i-nu'rus, the pilot of the ship of AEneas, "could not distinguish night from day, or remember his true course in the midst of the wave."

On the fourth day, however, the storm ceased and soon the Trojans sighted land in the distance. It was one of the islands of the Ionian sea, called the

Stroph'a-des. Here dwelt the Har'pies, monsters having faces like women, and bodies, wings, and claws like vultures. When the Trojans landed they saw herds of oxen and flocks of goats grazing in the fields. They killed some of them and prepared a feast upon the shore, and having first, in accordance with their invariable custom, made offerings to the gods, they proceeded "to banquet on the rich viands." But they had hardly begun their meal when the Harpies, with noisy flapping of wings and fearful cries, swooped down upon them, snatched off a great portion of the meat, and so spoiled the rest with their unclean touch that it was unfit to eat.

> From the mountain-tops with hideous cry,
> And clattering wings, the hungry Harpies fly:
> And snatch the meat, defiling all they find,
> And parting, leave a loathsome stench behind.
> DRYDEN, *AEneid*, BOOK III.

The Trojans got ready another meal and again sat down to eat, but the Harpies again came down upon them as before, and did in like manner. AEneas and his companions then resolved to fight, so they took their swords and drove the foul monsters off, though they could not kill any of them, for their skins were proof against wounds. One of them, however, remained behind, and perching on a rock, cried out in words of anger against the intruders. "Do you dare, base Trojans," said she, "to make war upon us after killing our oxen? Do you dare to drive the Harpies from the place which is their own? Listen then to what I have to tell you, which the father of the gods revealed to Phoe'bus Apollo, and Apollo revealed to me. Italy is the land you seek, and Italy you shall reach; but you shall not build the walls of your city until dire famine, visiting you because you have injured us, shall compel you to devour even your tables."

This Harpy was named Ce-lae'no. When the Trojans heard her awful words they prayed to the gods for protection, and then hastening to their ships, they put to sea. They soon came near Ith'a-ca, the island kingdom of Ulysses, the most skilful in stratagem of all the Greek chiefs at the Trojan war. Cursing the land which gave birth to that cruel enemy of their country, AEneas and his companions sailed past, and they continued their voyage until they reached the rocky island of Leu-ca'di-a on the coast of E-pi'rus, where there was another temple of Apollo. Here they landed, rejoicing that they had steered safely by so many cities of their enemies, for since leaving Crete their route had been mostly along the Grecian coast. They spent the winter in Leucadia, passing their leisure in games of wrestling and other athletic exercises, which were the sports of warriors in those ancient times. AEneas fastened to the door of the temple a shield of bronze—a trophy he had carried away from Troy—and upon it he put the inscription:

THIS ARMOR AENEAS WON FROM THE CONQUERING GREEKS.

In spring the wanderers again took to their ships, and sailing northwards, close to the coast, they came to Bu-thro'tum in Epirus, where they were surprised to learn that Hel'e-nus, son of Priam, was king of the country and that his wife was Androm'-a-che, who had formerly been wife of the famous Hector. AEneas having heard this upon landing, proceeded without delay towards the city, impatient to greet his kindred and to know how they had come to be there. It happened that just then Andromache was offering sacrifice on a tomb which she had erected outside the walls to the memory of Hector. Seeing AEneas approach she at once recognized him, but she was so overcome with surprise that for some time she was unable to utter a word. As soon as she recovered strength to speak she told AEneas that she had been carried off from Troy by Pyrrhus, and that Pyrrhus had given her to Helenus, after he himself had married Her-mi'o-ne, the daughter of the famous Helen. She also told that on the death of Pyrrhus who had been slain by O-res'tes, son of Agamemnon, part of his kingdom was given to Helenus.

Meanwhile king Helenus having heard of the arrival of the Trojans came out from the city to meet them, accompanied by a numerous train of attendants. He affectionately greeted AEneas and his companions, and invited them to his palace, where he hospitably entertained them during their stay. Helenus, besides being a king and the son of a king, was a famous soothsayer, so AEneas begged him to exercise his powers of prophecy on behalf of himself and his people. Helenus readily complied with the request. After offering the usual sacrifices to the gods, he told the Trojan chief that he had yet a long voyage to make before reaching his destination, that the place in which he should found his new kingdom was on the banks of a river, and that he would know it by finding there a white sow, with a litter of thirty young ones.

> "In the shady shelter of a wood,
> And near the margin of a gentle flood,
> Thou shalt behold a sow upon the ground,
> With thirty sucking young encompassed round
> (The dam and offspring white as falling snow);
> These on thy city shall their name bestow;
> And there shall end thy labors and thy woe."
> DRYDEN, *AEneid*, BOOK III.

As to the Harpy's dreadful prophecy that the Trojans would have to eat their tables, Helenus bade AEneas not to be troubled about it, for "the fates would find a way," and Apollo would be present to aid. Then the soothsayer warned his countrymen to shun the strait between Italy and Sicily, where on one side was the frightful monster Scyl'la, with the face of a woman and the tail of a dolphin, and on the other was the dangerous whirlpool Cha-ryb'dis. But more important than all other things, they must offer sacrifices and prayers to Juno, that her anger might be turned away from them, for she it was who had hitherto opposed all their efforts to reach their promised land.

Helenus also told them that on arriving in Italy they must seek out and consult the famous Sib'yl of Cu'mas. This was a prophetess who usually wrote her prophecies on leaves of trees, which she placed at the entrance to her cave. These leaves had to be taken up very carefully and quickly, for if they were scattered about by the wind, it would be impossible to put them in order again, so as to read them or understand their meaning. Helenus, therefore, directed AEneas to request the Sibyl to give her answers by word of mouth. She would do so, he said, and tell him all that was to happen to him and his people in Italy—the wars they would have to encounter, the dangers they were to meet, and how to avoid them.

Thus Helenus prophesied and gave counsel to his kinsmen. Then he made presents to AEneas and Anchises of valuable things in gold and silver, and he sent pilots to the ships, and horses and arms for the men. And Andromache gave embroidered robes to Ascanius and a cloak wrought in gold.

Soon afterwards the wanderers bade farewell to their friends, and set sail. Next day they came in sight of Italy, which they hailed with loud shouts of rejoicing. It was the south-eastern point of the peninsula, and as the Trojans approached it, they saw a harbor into which they ran their ships. Here they went ashore and offered sacrifices to Minerva, and also to Juno, remembering the advice of Helenus. But that part of the country being inhabited by Greeks, they made haste to depart, and taking their course southward, they passed by the Bay of Ta-ren'tum and down the coast until they came to the entrance of the strait now called Messina. This was a point of danger, for the loud roaring of the sea warned them that they were not far from the terrible Charybdis. Quickly Palinurus turned his ship to the left, and, all the others following, made straight for the Sicilian shore. Here they landed almost at the foot of AEtna, famous then as in our own times as a volcano or burning mountain. Under this mountain, according to an old legend, Jupiter imprisoned En-cel'a-dus, one of the giants who had dared to make war against heaven, and as often as the giant turned his weary sides, all Sicily trembled and the mountain sent forth flames of fire and streams of molten lava.

> Enceladus, they say, transfixed by Jove,
> With blasted limbs came tumbling from above;
> And when he fell, the avenging father drew
> This flaming hill, and on his body threw.
> As often as he turns his weary sides,
> He shakes the solid isle, and smoke, the heavens hides.
> DRYDEN, *AEneid*, BOOK III.

But beside the horrors of the "flaming hill" there was another danger to which the Trojans were now exposed. Sicily was the land of the terrible Cy'clops. These were fierce giants of immense size, with one eye, huge and round, in the middle of their foreheads. The morning after their arrival, the Trojans were surprised to see a stranger running forth from the woods, and with arms outstretched imploring their protection. Being asked who he was, he said he was a Greek, and that his name was Ach-e-men'ides. He had been at Troy with Ulysses, and was one of the companions of that famous warrior in his adventures after the siege. In their wanderings they had come to Sicily and had been in the very cave of Pol-y-phe'-mus, the largest and fiercest of the Cyclops, who had killed several of the unfortunate Greeks.

"I myself," said Achemenides, "saw him seize two of our number and break their bodies against a rock. I saw their limbs quivering between his teeth. But Ulysses did not suffer such things to go unpunished, for when the giant lay asleep, gorged with food, and made drunk with wine, (which Ulysses had given him) we, having prayed to the gods, and arranged by lot what part each should perform, crowded around him and with a sharp weapon bored out his eye, which was as large as the orb of the sun, and so we avenged the death of our comrades."

But in their flight from the cave, after punishing Polyphemus, the Greeks left Achemenides behind, and for three months he lived on berries in the woods. He now warned the Trojans to depart from the island with all speed, for, he said, a hundred other Cyclops, huge and savage, dwelt on those shores, tending their flocks among the hills.

> "Such, and so vast as Polypheme appears,
> A hundred more this hated island bears;
> Like him, in caves they shut their wooly sheep;
> Like him their herds on tops of mountains keep;
> Like him, with mighty strides they stalk from steep to steep."
> DRYDEN, *AEneid*, BOOK III

Scarcely had Achemenides finished his story when Polyphemus himself appeared coming down from the mountain in the midst of his flocks. A horrid monster he was, "huge, awful, hideous, ghastly, blind." In his hand he carried the trunk of a pine tree to guide his steps, and striding to the water's edge, he waded far into the sea, yet the waves did not touch his sides.

The Trojans now quickly got to their vessels, taking Achemenides with them, and they plied their oars with the utmost speed. Hearing the voices of the rowers and the sweep of their oars, the blind giant stretched out his hands in the direction of the sound, seeking to seize his enemies, as he took them to be. But the Trojans had got beyond his reach. Then in his rage and disappointment the monster raised a mighty shout which echoed from the mountain sides and brought forth his brethren from their woods and caves.

> "To heaven he lifts a monstrous roar,
>   Which sends a shudder through the waves,
> Shakes to its base the Italian shore,
>   And echoing runs through AEtna's caves.
> From rocks and woods the Cyclop host
> Rush startled forth, and crowd the coast.
> There glaring fierce we see them stand
> In idle rage, a hideous band,
> The sons of AEtna, carrying high
> Their towering summits to the sky."
>   CONINGTON, *AEneid*, BOOK III.

After thus escaping from the terrible Polyphemus, the Trojan wanderers sailed along the coasts of Sicily, and coming to the north-west extremity of the island, they put ashore at Drep'a-num. Here AEneas met with a misfortune which none of the prophets had predicted. This was the death of his venerable father Anchises.

> "After endless labors (often tossed
> By raging storms and driven on every coast),
> My dear, dear father, spent with age, I lost—
> Ease of my cares, and solace of my pain,
> Saved through a thousand toils, but saved in vain!
> The prophet, who my future woes revealed,
> Yet this, the greatest and the worst, concealed,
> And dire Celaeno, whose foreboding skill
> Denounced all else, was silent of this ill."
>   DRYDEN, *AEneid*, BOOK III.

III. A GREAT STORM—ARRIVAL IN CARTHAGE.

Thus far you have read the story of the Trojan exiles as it was told by AEneas himself to Di'do, queen of Carthage, at whose court we shall soon find him, after a dreadful storm which scattered his ships, sinking one, and driving the rest upon the coast of Africa. The narrative occupies the second and third books of the AEneid. In the first book the poet begins by telling of Juno's unrelenting hate, which was the chief cause of all the evils that befell the Trojans.

> Arms and the man I sing, who, forced by fate,
> And haughty Juno's unrelenting hate,
> Expelled and exiled, left the Trojan shore.
> Long labors, both by sea and land he bore.
> DRYDEN, *AEneid*, BOOK I.

It was at Juno's request that AE'o-lus, god of the winds, raised the great storm, just at the time when the wanderers, after leaving Drepanum, were about to direct their course towards the destined Hesperian land. For though AEneas and his companions, following the advice of Helenus, had offered prayers and sacrifices to the haughty goddess, still her anger was not appeased. She could not forget the judgment of Paris, or the prophecy that through the Trojan race was to come destruction on the city she loved. And so when she saw the ships of AEneas sailing towards the Italian coast, she gave vent to her anger in bitter words. "Must I then," said she, "desist from my purpose? Am I, the queen of heaven, not able to prevent the Trojans from establishing their kingdom in Italy? Who then will hereafter worship Juno or offer sacrifices on her altars?" With such thoughts inflaming her breast, the goddess hastened to AE-o'lia, the home of storms where dwelt AEolus, king of the winds. AEolia was one of the ancient names of the islands between Italy and Sicily, now known as the Lipari Islands. In a vast cave, in one of those islands king AEolus held the winds imprisoned and controlled their fury lest they should destroy the world—

> In a spacious cave of living stone,
> The tyrant AEolus, from his airy throne,
> With power imperial curbs the struggling winds,
> And sounding tempests in dark prisons binds:
> High in his hall the undaunted monarch stands,
> And shakes his sceptre, and their rage commands:
> Which did he not, their unresisted sway
> Would sweep the world before them in their way;
> Earth, air, and seas, through empty space would roll,
> And heaven would fly before the driving soul.
> In fear of this, the father of the gods
> Confined their fury to those dark abodes,
> And locked them safe within, oppressed with mountain loads;
> Imposed a king with arbitrary sway,
> To loose their fetters, or their force allay.
> DRYDEN, *AEneid*, BOOK I.

To this great king Juno appealed, begging him to send forth his storms against the ships of AEneas, and she promised to reward him by giving him in marriage the fair De-i-o-pe'a, most beautiful of all the nymphs or maids in her heavenly train of attendants. AEolus promptly replied saying that he was ready to obey the queen of heaven. "'Tis for you, O queen, to command and for me to execute your will."

Then AEolus struck the side of the cavern with his mighty scepter, whereupon the rock flew open and the winds rushed furiously forth. In an instant a terrific hurricane swept over land and sea. The lightning flashed, the thunder pealed, and the waves rolled mountain high around the Trojan fleet.

> All in a moment sun and skies
> Are blotted from the Trojans' eyes;
> Black night is brooding o'er the deep,
> Sharp thunder peals, live lightnings leap;
> The stoutest warrior holds his breath,
> And looks as on the face of death.
>   CONINGTON, *AEneid*, BOOK I.

Filled with terror, AEneas bewailed his unhappy fate, and lamented that it had not been his lot to fall with those

> Who died at Troy like valiant men
>   E'en in their parents' view.

But the storm increased in fury. Three of his ships were dashed against hidden rocks, while before his eyes one went down with all its crew.

> And here and there above the waves were seen
> Arms, pictures, precious goods and floating men.
>   DRYDEN, *AEneid*, BOOK I.

Meantime the roaring of wind and waves had reached the ears of Neptune, in his coral palace beneath the sea. Neptune was one of the gods who were friendly to AEneas, and so when he raised his head above the waters, and beheld the ships scattered about and the hero himself in deep distress, the ocean king was very angry. Instantly he summoned the winds before him, and sternly rebuked them for daring to cause such disturbance in his dominions without his authority. Then he ordered them to depart forthwith to their caverns, and tell their master that not to him belonged the kingdom of the sea.

> "Back to your master instant flee,
> And tell him, not to him but me
> The imperial trident of the sea

>   Fell by the lot's award."
>   CONINGTON, *AEneid*, BOOK I.

It was by lot that the empire of the universe had been divided among the three brothers Jupiter, Neptune and Pluto, the kingdom of the ocean falling to Neptune, the heavens to Jupiter and the "lower regions" or regions of the dead to Pluto. Neptune, therefore, had full power within his own dominion, and so the winds had to retire at his command. Then immediately the sea became calm and still, and AEneas with seven ships—all that he could find of his fleet—sailed for the African coast, which was the nearest land, the storm having driven them far out of their course. Soon discovering a suitable harbor, deep in a bay, with high rocks on each side at the entrance, the tempest-tossed Trojans gladly put ashore, and lighting a fire on the beach, they prepared a meal of parched corn, which they ground with stones.

Meanwhile AEneas climbed a rock and looked out over the sea hoping to catch sight of some of the lost vessels. He was accompanied by his armor-bearer A-cha'tes, who was so devoted to his chief that the name is often used to signify a very faithful friend. But they could see none of the missing ships and so they returned to their companions. Then AEneas delivered an address to his people, bidding them be of good cheer, and reminding them of the decree of heaven that they should have a peaceful settlement in La'ti-um—that fair Italian land, to which the gods would surely guide them in due time.

> "Comrades and friends! for ours is strength
>   Has brooked the test of woes;
> O worse-scarred hearts! these wounds at length
>   The lgods will heal, like those.
> You that have seen grim Scylla rave,
>   And heard her monsters yell,
> You that have looked upon the cave
>   Where savage Cyclops dwell,
> Come, cheer your souls, your fears forget;
> This suffering will yield us yet
>   A pleasant tale to tell.
> Through chance, through peril lies our way
> To Latium, where the fates display
> A mansion of abiding stay;
> There Troy her fallen realm shall raise;
> Bear up and live for happier days."
>   CONINGTON, *AEneid*, BOOK I.

It is not to be supposed that all this time the goddess Venus was forgetful of the sufferings of her son. Even while AEneas was thus speaking to his fellow wanderers she was pleading his cause before the throne of Jupiter himself on the top of Mount Olympus. "What offence, O king of heaven," said she, "has my AEneas committed? How have the Trojans offended? What is to be the end of their sufferings? Are they to be forever persecuted on account of the anger of one goddess?"

To this appeal the king of the gods answered assuring Venus that the promises made to the Trojan exiles should all be fulfilled. AEneas, he said, should make war against fierce tribes in Italy, and conquer them, and rule in La-vin'i-um. After him his son Iulus should reign for thirty years, and build a city to be called Alba Longa, where his descendants would hold sovereign power for three hundred years. Then from the same race should come Rom'u-lus, who would found the city Rome, which would in time conquer Greece and rule the world.

> "The people Romans call, the city Rome
> To them no bounds of empire I assign,
> Nor term of years to their immortal line,
> E'en haughty Juno, who, with endless broils,
> Earth, seas, and heaven, and Jove himself turmoils,
> At length atoned, her friendly power shall join,
> To cherish and advance the Trojan line.
> An age is ripening in revolving fate,
> When Troy shall overturn the Grecian state,
> And sweet revenge her conquering sons shall call
> To crush the people that conspired her fall,
> Then Caesar from the Julian stock shall rise,
> Whose empire ocean, and whose fame the skies
> Alone shall bound."
>   DRYDEN, *AEneid*, BOOK I.

Thus did the king of heaven prophesy the future greatness and power of the Julian line. Then he sent Mercury, the messenger of the gods, down to earth to bid the queen of Carthage and her people give a hospitable reception to the Trojans, for it was near that city, on the Li'by-an shore, that they had landed after the storm. Venus herself, too, came down from Olympus, and, in the garb of a huntress, appeared to her son and the faithful Achates, as they were exploring the coast to find out what land it was, and by what people possessed. She did not make herself known to them, but inquired if they had seen one of her sisters who had strayed away from her. AEneas answered: "None of your sisters have we seen, O virgin, or shall we call you goddess, for such you seem to be? Whoever you are, graciously relieve our anxiety by informing us what country this is into which unkind fortune has driven us.

> "Instruct us 'neath what sky at last,
> Upon what shore our lot is cast;
> We wander here by tempest blown,
> The people and the place unknown."
>   CONINGTON, *AEneid*, BOOK I.

To these inquiries Venus, still maintaining her disguise, replied by telling the Trojan heroes the story of Carthage and Queen Dido. This famous woman was the daughter of Be'lus, king of Tyre, a city of Phoe-nic'i-a, in Asia Minor. She married a wealthy Tyrian lord named Si-chae'us. On her father's death, her brother Pyg-ma'li-on became king of Tyre. He was a cruel and avaricious tyrant, and in order to get possession of his brother-in-law's riches, he had him put to death, concealing the crime from his sister by many false tales. But in a dream the ghost of Sichaeus appeared to Dido and told her of the wicked deed of Pygmalion. He at the same time advised her to fly from the country with all speed, and he informed her of the place where he had hidden his treasures—a large sum in gold and silver, which he bade her take to help her in her flight.

Dido therefore got together a number of ships, and put to sea accompanied by a number of her countrymen who hated the cruel tyrant. They sailed to the coast of Africa and landed in Libya, where they purchased from the inhabitants as much ground as could be encompassed by a bull's hide cut into thongs. Then they commenced to build a city which they called Carthage, and even now they were engaged in raising its walls.

Such was the story of Dido which Venus related to AEneas and Achates. Having concluded, she inquired in her turn who they were, from what country they had come, and whither they were going. In reply AEneas gave a brief account of his wanderings since the fall of Troy. Then the goddess directed him to go into the city and present himself before the queen, and she pointed to an augury in the sky—twelve swans flying above their heads—which, she said, was a sign that the ships they had supposed to be lost were at that moment sailing into the harbor.

So saying Venus turned to leave them, when suddenly a marvelous change took place in her dress and appearance, so that AEneas knew she was his mother, and he cried to her to permit him to touch her hand and speak with her as her son. The goddess, however, made no answer, but she cast over Aeneas and his companion a thick veil of cloud so that no one might see or molest them on their way. Thus rendered invisible, they went towards the city. When they reached it they found a great many men at work, some finishing the walls, others erecting great buildings of various kinds. In the center of the town was a magnificent temple of Juno.

> Enriched with gifts, and with a golden shrine;
> But more the goddess made the place divine.
> On brazen steps the marble threshold rose,
> And brazen plates the cedar beams enclose;
> The rafters are with brazen coverings crowned;
> The lofty doors on brazen hinges sound.
> DRYDEN, *AEneid*, BOOK I.

Entering this temple, AEneas was astonished to find the walls covered with paintings representing scenes of the Trojan war.

> He saw, in order painted on the wall,
> Whatever did unhappy Troy befall;
> The wars that fame around the world had blown,
> All to the life, and every leader known.
> He stopped, and weeping said: "O friend! e'en here!
> The monuments of Trojan woes appear!"
> DRYDEN, *AEneid*, BOOK I.

Amongst the pictures, AEneas recognized one of himself performing deeds of valor in the thick of the fight. While he and his companion, both still invisible, were gazing with admiration upon those scenes Queen Dido came into the temple, attended by a numerous train of warriors, and took her seat upon a high-raised throne. Presently there appeared a number of Trojans advancing towards the queen, and AEneas rejoiced to see that they were some of his own people belonging to the ships that had been separated from him during the storm. They had been cast ashore on a different part of the coast, and not hearing of the safe arrival of AEneas, they were now come to beg the help and protection of Dido. Having heard their story, which Il-i'o-neus, one of their number, briefly related, the queen bade them dismiss their fears, promising that she would give them whatever assistance they needed, and send out messengers to search the Libyan coasts for their leader AEneas. But at this point the mist that encompassed AEneas and his companion suddenly vanished and the hero stood forth, beheld by all, his face resembling that of a god.

> The Trojan chief appeared in open sight
> August in visage, and serenely bright.
> His mother-goddess, with her hands divine,
> Had formed his curling locks, and made his temples shine,
> And given his rolling eyes a sparkling grace,
> And breathed a youthful vigor on his face.
> DRYDEN, *AEneid*, BOOK I.

AEneas now made himself known to the queen and thanked her for her kindness to his people. Dido was astonished at the sudden appearance of the hero, of whom she had already heard much. Her father, Belus, she said, had told her of the fall of Troy and of the name of AEneas, and having herself suffered many misfortunes, she had learned to have pity for the distressed.

> "For I myself, like you, have been distressed;
> Till heaven afforded me this place of rest;
> Like you, an alien in a land unknown,
> I learn to pity woes so like my own."
> DRYDEN, *AEneid*, BOOK I.

Then she invited the hero into the royal apartments where a grand banquet was prepared in his honor. She also caused a supply of provisions to be taken to his people on the shore—twenty oxen, a hundred swine, and a hundred fat lambs. Meanwhile AEneas sent Achates to bring his son Ascanius to the city, bidding him at the same time to take with him presents for the queen, costly and beautiful things that had been saved from the ruins of Troy—a mantle embroidered with gold, a scepter which had belonged to I-li'o-ne, King Priam's daughter, and a necklace strung with pearls.

At the banquet Queen Dido sat on a golden couch, surrounded by the Trojan chiefs and her Tyrian lords. By her side was seated the handsome youth whom Achates had brought from the ships as the son of AEneas. Dido admired the beautiful boy and fondled him in her arms little thinking that it was Cupid, the god of love, whom Venus had sent to the banquet under the appearance of Iulus.

> Unhappy Dido little thought what guest,
> How dire a god she drew so near her breast.
> DRYDEN, *AEneid*, BOOK I.

The real Ascanius meantime lay in peaceful slumber in a sacred grove in the island of Cyprus, to which Venus had borne him away.

> Lulled in her lap, amidst a train of Loves,
> She gently bears him to her blissful groves;
> Then with a wreath of myrtle crowns his head,
> And softly lays him on a flowery bed.
> DRYDEN, AEneid BOOK 1.

And so Queen Dido entertained the chiefs of Troy and of Carthage, with the god of love seated beside her on her golden couch. A hundred maids and as many pages attended upon the guests. After the viands were removed, I-o'pas, the Tyrian minstrel and poet, played upon his gilded lyre, and sang about the wondrous things in the heavens and on earth.

> The various labors of the wandering moon,
> And whence proceed the eclipses of the sun;
> The original of men and beasts; and whence
> The rains arise, and fires their warmth dispense;
> What shakes the solid earth; what cause delays
> The summer nights, and shortens winter days.
> DRYDEN, AEneid. BOOK I.

The song of Iopas was applauded by the entire assemblage. Then Queen Dido after asking Aeneas many questions about Priam and Hector, and Achilles, and Memnon, and Diomede and other heroes of the Trojan war, begged him to tell the whole story from the beginning. "Come, my guest," said she, "relate to us from the very first the stratagems of the Greeks, the adventures of your friends, and your own wanderings."

It was in compliance with this request that Aeneas, as has been said, recounted the history (already given) of the ruin of Troy, and of his own misfortunes, commencing with the artifice of the wooden horse, and ending with the storm which drove his ships upon the Carthaginian coast. The events of the story extended over a period of seven years, for it was now that length of time since the fatal "peace offering" brought destruction on the city of Priam.

IV. DIDO'S LOVE—THE FUNERAL GAMES—SHIPS BURNED BY THE WOMEN.

Queen Dido was much interested in the story told by Aeneas, but more so in the hero himself. His many virtues, the honors and glories of his race, made a strong impression on her mind; his looks and words were imprinted on her heart. In short, the Carthaginian queen was in love with the Trojan prince. She confided her secret to her sister Anna, and she said that if she had not vowed, on the death of her dear husband Sichaeus, never again to unite with any one in the bond of marriage, she might think of giving her hand to her noble guest.

Sister Anna knew that such a marriage would be a great advantage to Carthage, which might need brave defenders like the Trojans, since there were many warlike princes in that part of Africa, who might some time attack the new city. And if the Trojan arms were joined to those of Carthage, both would be strong enough to resist the most powerful enemy, and the new kingdom would become great and flourishing. "Let us therefore," said she, "pray to the gods for help and at the same time endeavor by all means to detain our Trojan guests as long as possible upon our shore."

The queen listened to her sister's advice with pleasure, more especially as it was in accord with her own feelings. Her scruples about a second marriage soon vanished, and so she continued to entertain the Trojans and their chief with princely hospitality.

> And now she leads the Trojan chief along
> The lofty walls, amidst the busy throng;
> Displays her Tyrian wealth, and rising town,
> Which love, without his labor makes his own.
> This pomp she shows, to tempt her wandering guest:
> Her faltering tongue forbids to speak the rest.
> When day declines and feasts renew the night,
> Still on his face she feeds her famished sight;
> She longs again to hear the prince relate
> His own adventures, and the Trojan fate.
> He tells it o'er and o'er; but still in vain;
> For still she begs to hear it once again.
>   DRYDEN, *AEneid*, BOOK IV

Meanwhile the goddess Juno, watching the course of events, also saw the advantage, to her favorite city, of a union with the Trojan chief. If he and his people, she thought, could be persuaded to settle in Carthage, that city and not the long talked of Rome, would come to be the center of power and the ruler of the world. She therefore proposed to Venus a treaty of "eternal peace" on the condition of a marriage between Aeneas and Dido.

> "Your Trojan with my Tyrian let us join;
> So Dido shall be yours, AEneas mine—
> One common kingdom, one united line."
>   DRYDEN, *AEneid*, BOOK IV.

Venus was not at all deceived by this plausible speech. She well understood the motive and purpose of Juno to secure future power and glory for Carthage and divert from Rome the empire of the world, nevertheless she answered in mild words saying, "Who could be so foolish as to reject such an alliance, and prefer to be at war with the queen of heaven? Yet there is a difficulty. I do not know whether it is the pleasure of Jupiter that the Tyrians and Trojans should dwell together in one city. Will he approve the union of the two nations? Perhaps, however, you, who are his wife, may be able to induce him to do so. It is for you, then, to lead the way, and where you lead I shall follow."

But another obstacle stood in the way of Juno's proposed alliance. There was at that time a certain African king named I-ar'bas, a very important personage, for he was a son of Jupiter. It was from him that Dido when she first came to Libya had bought the ground to build her city. Now Iarbas wished to have Dido for his wife, and he had asked her to marry him, but she had refused. Great was his anger, therefore, when he heard that the Trojan chief had been received and honored in Carthage and that a marriage between him and the queen was talked of as a certain thing. So he went to the temple of his father Jupiter, and complained bitterly of the conduct of Dido in rejecting himself and taking a foreign prince into her kingdom to be its ruler. The king of heaven, naturally enough sympathising with his son, gave ear to his complaint and he forthwith dispatched Mercury with a message to AEneas, bidding him to depart instantly from Carthage. This command the swift-winged god, having sped down from Olympus, and sought out the Trojan hero, delivered in impressive words.

> "All powerful Jove
> Who sways the world below and heaven above,
> Has sent me down with this severe command:
> What means thy lingering in the Libyan land?
> If glory cannot move a mind so mean,
> Nor future praise from flitting pleasure wean,
> Regard the fortunes of thy rising heir:
> The promised crown let young Ascanius wear,
> To whom the Ausonian sceptre, and the state
> Of Rome's imperial name, is owed by fate."
> DRYDEN, *AEneid*, BOOK IV.

The command filled AEneas with astonishment and fear. He knew that he must obey, but how could he break the intelligence to Dido, or what excuse could he offer for so sudden a departure?

> What should he say, or how should he begin?
> What course alas! remains, to steer between
> The offended lover and the powerful queen.
> DRYDEN, *AEneid*, BOOK IV.

There being, however, no middle course, Aeneas directed his chiefs to get ready the ships, call together the crews, and prepare their arms, and to do all as quietly and secretly as possible. Meanwhile he himself would watch for a favorable opportunity of obtaining the queen's consent to their departure.

> Himself, meantime, the softest hours would choose,
> Before the love-sick lady heard the news,
> And move her tender mind, by slow degrees

To suffer what the sovereign power decrees.
 DRYDEN, *AEneid*, BOOK IV.

But Dido soon discovered what the Trojans were about, and she sent for AEneas and reproached him in angry words for his deception and ingratitude. Then her anger gave way to grief and tears, and she implored him to alter his resolution, declaring that if he would thus suddenly leave her she must surely die. AEneas was in deep distress at the spectacle of the sorrowing queen, yet he dared not yield to her entreaties, since it was the decree of the fates and the command of Jupiter that he should remain no longer in Carthage.

The Trojans therefore hastened their preparations and were soon ready to set sail; but there came another warning conveyed to them by the god Mercury, who, while AEneas was asleep in his ship, appeared to him in a dream, bidding him to speed away that very night, for if he waited until morning he would find the harbor filled with queen Dido's fleet to prevent his departure. Starting from his couch AEneas quickly roused his companions and gave the order for instantly putting to sea.

 "Haste to your oars! your crooked anchors weigh,
 And speed your flying sails, and stand to sea!
 A god commands! he stood before my sight,
 And urged me once again to speedy flight."
 DRYDEN, *AEneid*, BOOK IV.

Promptly the order of the chief was obeyed, and soon the Trojan vessels were sailing away from the city of Dido. And at dawn of morning the unhappy queen, looking forth from her watch tower, beheld them far out at sea. Then she prayed that there might be eternal enmity between the descendants of AEneas and the people of Carthage, and that a man would come of her nation who would persecute the Trojan race with fire and sword.

 "These are my prayers, and this my dying will;
 And you, my Tyrians, every curse fulfill:
 Perpetual hate and mortal wars proclaim
 Against the prince, the people, and the name.
 These grateful offerings on my grave bestow;
 Nor league, nor love, the hostile nations know!
 Now and from hence in every future age,
 When rage excites your arms, and strength supplies the rage,
 Rise some avenger of our Libyan blood;
 With fire and sword pursue the perjured brood:
 Our arms, our seas, our shores, opposed to theirs;

And the same hate descend on all our heirs!"
  DRYDEN, *AEneid*, BOOK IV.

Vergil thus makes Dido prophesy the long conflict between Rome and Carthage, (known as the Punic wars) and the achievements of the famous Carthaginian general, Han'ni-bal, who carried the war into the heart of Italy (218 B. C.) and defeated the Romans in several great battles.

In her grief at the departure of AEneas, the unhappy queen resolved to put an end to her life. She bade her servants erect in the inner court yard of her palace a lofty pile of wood, called a funeral pyre, and upon it to place an image of AEneas as well as the arms he had left behind him. Then mounting the pyre, to which flaming torches had been applied, she stabbed herself with her false lover's sword, and so died.

The Trojans from their ships, saw the smoke and flame ascending from the palace of Dido. They knew not the cause, yet AEneas, suspecting what had happened, deeply lamented the fate of the unhappy queen.

  The cause unknown; yet his presaging mind
  The fate of Dido from the fire divined.
  Dire auguries from hence the Trojans draw;
  Till neither fires nor shining shores they saw.
    DRYDEN, *AEneid*, BOOK IV.

The fleet was no sooner out of sight of the Libyan coast than the pilot Palinurus observed signs of a storm. He proposed, therefore, that they should make for the Sicilian shore, which was not far distant. AEneas gladly consented, for he wished to stand again upon the spot where his father's bones were laid. Moreover the good king A-ces'tes, who ruled in that part of the island, was a Trojan by descent, and he had hospitably received the wanderers on their former visit. They, therefore, turned the prows of their galleys towards Sicily, and soon reached Drepanum, where they were met and welcomed by Acestes, who from a hill top had seen their vessels approaching the shore.

Next day AEneas, accompanied by king Acestes, and a great multitude of people, proceeded to the grave of Anchises where they erected altars, and according to the custom of the times, poured wine and milk on the ground, as an offering to the gods. Fresh flowers were then scattered on the tomb. While these ceremonies were being performed all present were startled by the appearance of a huge serpent with scales of golden hue, which suddenly glided from beneath the tomb, trailed among the bowls or goblets containing the wine and milk, tasted slightly of the contents, and then returned into the vault.

> Betwixt the rising altars, and around,
> The sacred monster shot along the ground;
> With harmless play amidst the bowls he passed,
> And with his lolling tongue assayed the taste:
> Thus fed with holy food, the wondrous guest
> Within the hollow tomb retired to rest.
> DRYDEN, *AEneid*, BOOK V.

AEneas believed that this serpent was an attendant on the shade of Anchises. He supposed, therefore, that his father was now elevated to the dignity of a god, for most of the gods had inferior deities assigned to them as ministers or messengers.

Besides the sacrifices and other ceremonies at the tomb, there were games and athletic exercises in honor of Anchises, this also being one of the customs of the ancients in paying tribute to the memory of their dead heroes. The principal event in the games was a ship race in which the most skilful of the Trojan mariners took part. In this contest Mnes'theus with a ship named *Pristis*, and Clo-an'-thus commanding the *Scylla* performed wonderful feats of seamanship. So equally were they matched and so well did they manage their vessels that both would probably have reached the goal or winning post together, had it not been for the interference of the gods. The goal was a branch of an oak tree fixed to a small rock in the bay facing the beach on which the spectators were assembled. As the *Scylla* was approaching the rock on the home run, the *Pristis*, which had been pressing close behind, shot alongside, and was almost beak to beak with its competitor. Then Cloanthus stretching forth his arms to heaven, prayed the gods of the sea to help him at that critical moment, promising that he would offer sacrifices of thanksgiving on their altars, if he should win the race. His prayer was quickly heard. From their palaces in the deep, the Ne-re'ids, Neptune's band of attendants and assistants, rushed to his aid, and with his mighty hand Por-tu'nus, the god of harbors, coming behind the *Scylla*, pushed the vessel along, speeding her forward more swiftly than the wind.

> And old Portunus with his breadth of hand,
> Pushed on and sped the galley to the land,
> Swift as a shaft, or winged wind, she flies,
> And darting to the port, obtains the prize.
> DRYDEN, *AEneid*, BOOK V.

Cloanthus was declared victor and received the first prize—a rich mantle embroidered in gold. The second prize was given to Mnestheus, and suitable rewards were also bestowed on the crews. After the ship race AEneas and the vast multitude of Trojans and Sicilians proceeded to a grassy plain not far from the shore where the other games were held. The first was a foot race in which a large number took part. Among them were Eu-ry'a-lus and Ni'sus, Trojan youths famed for their mutual friendship, and Di-o'res, a young prince of Priam's royal line. Among the Sicilian competitors were Sa'li-us and Pa'tron, and two young men, El'y-mus and Pan'o-pes, companions of King Acestes.

[Illustration with caption: THE FOOT RACE. (Drawn by Birch)]

The signal having been given, the racers darted off like lightning. Nisus quickly took the lead springing far away ahead of the rest. Next, but at a long distance came Salius, and after him Euryalus, followed by Elymus, with Diores close by his side. Nisus would have reached the goal first, but just as he was approaching it, he lost his foothold at a slippery spot on the course, and fell headlong upon the ground. Seeing then that it was not possible for him to win, he thought of his friend Euryalus, and rising from the ground he set himself right in the way of Salius who was rushing forward.

> E'en then affection claims its part;
> Euryalus is in his heart;
> Uprising from the sodden clay,
> He casts himself in Salius' way,
> And Salius tripped and sprawling lay.
> CONINGTON, *AEneid*, BOOK V.

This gave the victory to Euryalus, but Salius protested against the foul play by which he had been defeated, and claimed that he was entitled to the first prize. AEneas, however, decided that the prize should go to him who had actually reached the goal first. Nevertheless, he gave Salius a lion's hide, heavy with shaggy fur and gilt claws. Nisus, too, claimed a reward, and AEneas sympathising with his misfortune, presented to him a shield of beautiful workmanship, which had been taken from the pillars of Neptune's temple in the city of Troy.

Games of boxing and archery—shooting with bows and arrows—came next. In the latter contest, king Acestes and Mnestheus took part. The other competitors were Eu-ry'ti-on and Hip-poc'o-on. For a mark to shoot at, they tied a pigeon to the top of a tall mast set firmly in the ground. Hippocoon won the first chance in the drawing of lots. His arrow struck the mast with such force that it fixed itself in the wood. The arrow of Mnestheus broke the cord by which the pigeon was attached to the mast, and as she flew off, Eurytion discharged his shaft with so true an aim that it killed the bird. Acestes, who had drawn the last lot, now fired, though there was nothing to shoot at, but his arrow as it winged its way high into the air, presented to the spectators a marvelous sight.

> E'en in the mid expanse of skies
> The arrow kindles as it flies,
> Behind it draws a fiery glare,
> Then wasting, vanishes in air.
>   CONINGTON, *AEneid*, BOOK V.

AEneas interpreted this wonderful event as a sign of the will of the gods that Acestes should receive the honors of victory, and so he presented to him a goblet embossed in gold, which bad belonged to his father Anchises. But prizes were given to Eurytion also and to the other archers. Then followed the last of the games of the day, a grand exhibition of horsemanship, in which a number of the Trojan youth,— chief amongst them the boy Iulus,—took the leading part.

Thus did AEneas pay honor to his father's memory. Meantime the unrelenting Juno was devising schemes to prevent the hero and his companions from reaching their promised land. With this object she sent her messenger I'ris down to the Trojan women, who sat together on the shore while the men were assembled at their games, for at these exercises females were not allowed to be spectators. As the women sat on the beach, looking out upon the sea, they thought and talked of the hardships they had endured during their long wanderings, and lamented their wretched lot in having still so much to suffer before they could find permanent homes to settle in.

> "Alas! (said one) what oceans yet remain
> For us to sail! what labors to sustain!"
> All take the word, and, with a general groan
> Implore the gods for peace, and places of their own.
>   DRYDEN, *AEneid*, BOOK V.

Iris joined in these complaints, and they thought she was one of themselves, for she had assumed the appearance and dress of a Trojan, and pretended to be Ber'o-e, a Trojan woman who was just then on a sick bed in her own chamber. "Unhappy are we," cried the false Beroe; "far better for us would it have been if we had died by the hands of the Greeks before the walls of our native city! What miserable doom does fortune reserve for us? The seventh year since the destruction of Troy has already passed, and yet, after having wandered over so many lands and seas, we still pursue an ever-fleeing Italy; and we are tossed on the waves. Why should we not settle here in Sicily? Come then and let us burn those cursed ships. For in my sleep the prophetess Cassandra seemed to present me with flaming brands and to say, 'Seek here for a new Troy, here is your home.' Therefore let there be no further delay. Now is the time for action."

With these words she seized a brand from a fire on an altar close by, and hurled it towards the ships. But at this point one of the women, Pyr'go by name, who had just then joined the party, discovered that it was not Beroe who had been speaking, for she recognized in the eyes and voice and gait, the resemblance of a goddess.

> "No Beroe, matrons, have you here,
> See, breathing in her face appear
>   Signs of celestial life;
> Observe her eyes, how bright they shine;
> Mien, accent, walk are all divine.
> Beroe herself I left but now
> Sick and outworn, with clouded brow,
> That she alone should fail to pay
> Due reverence to Anchises' day."
>   CONINGTON, *AEneid*, BOOK V

As Pyrgo ceased speaking, Iris, assuming her own form, mounted into the sky. Then the Trojan women, astonished at what they had seen, and excited almost to madness, cried out with a loud voice, and, seizing brands from the altars, they rushed to the ships.

> They shriek aloud; they snatch with impious hands
> The food of altars; firs and flaming brands,
> Green boughs and saplings, mingled in their haste,
> And smoking torches, on the ships they cast.
>   DRYDEN, *AEneid*, BOOK V.

The ships were now on fire and the alarm quickly reaching the men, they rushed to the shore and endeavored to subdue the flames, while the women already regretting their folly, fled in terror from the scene. But in spite of the efforts of the men the fire rapidly spread, and it seemed as if the entire Trojan fleet was doomed to destruction. Then the pious AEneas, with upraised hands, prayed to Jupiter for help, and immediately there came a great rain-storm, and the water descended in torrents, until every spark was extinguished. Four of the ships, however, were destroyed.

AEneas was much distressed by this misfortune, and he began to think that it might be better, even in disregard of the fates, and the prophecies, to remain in Sicily, than to make any further attempt to reach the promised Italian land. But one of his people, an old and a very wise man, named Nau'tes, strongly urged that the will of the gods ought to be obeyed. As to those who were weary of the enterprise—the aged, the feeble, and such of the women as were not willing to undergo further fatigues at sea-he advised that they should be left under the protection of Acestes, who, being himself of Trojan blood, would doubtless grant them a settlement in his kingdom.

> "Your friend Acestes is of Trojan kind;
> To him disclose the secrets of your mind;
> Here you may build a common town for all,
> And, from Acestes' name, Acesta call."
>   DRYDEN, *AEneid*, BOOK V.

While AEneas was still in doubt what course to pursue, his father appeared to him in a dream and bade him do as Nautes had advised. Acestes willingly consented, and so a Trojan colony was formed in Sicily, and AEneas marked out with a plow the boundaries of the new city, which he called after the king's name. Soon afterwards preparations for departure were made, and AEneas set sail, accompanied by all of his people who were still willing to follow his fortunes, and strong enough to endure further toils and hardships.

They had a safe voyage to Italy, for Venus had entreated Neptune to protect her son and his fleet.

The god of the ocean was favorable, and he promised to take care that the Trojans should reach their destination in safety. But there was to be one exception. "One life," he said, "shall be given for many." The victim was the famous pilot Palinurus, and the poet tells us that his fate was brought about by the action of Som'nus, the god of sleep.

This god taking upon himself the likeness of Phor'bas, one of the sons of Priam, who was killed during the Trojan war, appeared to Palinurus during one of the watches of the night, and tried to persuade him to lie down and sleep, while he himself would stand at the helm and steer the ship. But Palinurus refused to quit his post. Then the treacherous god waved before his eyes a branch that had been dipped in the Stygian Le'the, the fabled river of forgetfulness, and soon the pilot dropped off into a deep slumber, during which Somnus leaning heavily upon him, plunged him headlong into the waves.

AEneas was deeply grieved at the loss of his faithful pilot. He himself took charge of the ship, and the whole fleet, secure under the protection of Neptune, reached the Italian coast without further mishap.

V. THE SIBYL OF CUMAE—THE GOLDEN BOUGH—IN THE REGIONS OF THE DEAD.

AEneas was now in Italy, but not in the part of it where the destined city was to be founded. The prophet, Helenus, as we have seen, had directed him that when he reached the Hesperian land he should visit the Cu-mae'an Sibyl, and learn from her what difficulties he was yet to encounter, and how to overcome them. Cumae, where the Sibyl dwelt, was on the coast of Campa'ni-a, and to this place, therefore, AEneas directed his course after leaving

Sicily. Having safely landed, the hero lost no time in making his way to the temple of Apollo, for in a cave adjoining this temple and communicating with it by a hundred doors and as many avenues or corridors, the Sibyl gave her answers.

There were many sibyls in ancient times. The most celebrated was the Sibyl of Cumae. She had several names, but the one adopted by Vergil is Deiph'o-be. Apollo once fell in love with this Sibyl and he promised to give her whatever she should ask if she would marry him. Deiphobe asked to live as many years as she had grains of sand in her hand at the time. She forgot, however, to ask for the continuance of health and youth, of which she was then in possession. Apollo granted her request but she refused to perform her part of the bargain, and soon afterwards she became aged and feeble. She had already lived seven hundred years when AEneas came into Italy, and she had three centuries more to live before her years would be as numerous as the grains of sand which she had held in her hand.

As AEneas with several of his companions approached the cave, they were met at the outer entrance by the Sibyl herself. Then the Trojan hero, after a prayer to Apollo, begged the good will of the prophetess that her answers might be favorable to him and his people.

> "And thou, O sacred maid, inspired to see
> The event of things in dark futurity!
> Give me, what heaven has promised to my fate,
> To conquer and command the Latian state;
> To fix my wandering gods, and find a place
> For the long exiles of the Trojan race."
>   DRYDEN, *AEneid*, BOOK VI.

Nor did AEneas forget to beg the Sibyl, as Helenus had directed him, to give her revelations by word of mouth, and not on leaves of trees, as was her custom.

> "But, oh! commit not thy prophetic mind
> To flitting leaves, the sport of every wind,
> Lest they disperse in air our empty fate;
> Write not, but, what the powers ordain, relate."
>   DRYDEN, *AEneid*, BOOK VI.

The Sibyl graciously consented, and then the spirit of prophecy having moved her, she told AEneas of the dangers that yet lay before him, dangers far more formidable than any he had hitherto encountered.

> "Escaped the dangers of the watery reign,
> Yet more and greater ills by land remain.
> The coast so long desired (nor doubt the event),

Thy troops shall reach, but, having reached, repent.
Wars! horrid wars, I view!—a field of blood,
And Tiber rolling with a purple flood."
DRYDEN, *AEneid*, BOOK VI.

But AEneas was not discouraged by this terrible prophecy. He was ready, he said, to meet the worst that could come, and now he was about to undertake an enterprise more arduous than any the soothsayers had told him of. This was a descent into the regions of Pluto—the land of the dead—to visit the shade of his father, who in a dream had requested him to do so, telling him that the Cumaean Sibyl would be his guide, for the entrance to the Lower World was near Lake A-ver'nus, not far from the cave of the prophetess.

AEneas, therefore, entreated the Sibyl to consent to be his conductor that so he might comply with his father's wish. In reply to this request the prophetess warned the Trojan chief that the undertaking was one of great danger. The descent into the kingdom of Pluto, she said, was easy, but, to return to the upper world—that was a task difficult for mortals to accomplish. Few there were who had entered the gloomy realms of Dis, to whom it had been permitted ever to retrace their steps.

"The journey down to the abyss
  Is prosperous and light;
The palace-gates of gloomy Dis
  Stand open day and night;
But upward to retrace the way
And pass into the light of day,
There comes the stress of labor; this
  May task a hero's might."
CONINGTON, *AEneid*, BOOK VI.

Nevertheless if AEneas were still determined on this perilous journey she was willing to aid him and be his guide. But one thing, she said, must first be done. In the woods around the cave was a tree on which grew a bough with leaves and twigs of gold.

No mortal could enter Hades without this bough to present to Pro-ser'pi-na, the queen of Pluto. When the bough was torn off, a second, also of gold, immediately sprung up. It had to be sought for diligently, and when discovered it had to be grasped firmly with the hand. If the fates should be favorable to the enterprise, the bough could be plucked easily; otherwise, the strength of man could not tear it from the tree, nor could it be lopped off even with the sharpest sword.

Here was a formidable difficulty. How was AEneas to find out the wonderful tree? The Sibyl told him only that it was in the woods, and the searching might be long and fruitless. But again his never-failing friend came to his aid. While he was searching the wood with some of his companions, two doves suddenly appeared, and alighted on the ground before them. AEneas knew that they had come from his goddess-mother, the dove being the favorite bird of Venus.

> He knew his mother's birds; and thus he prayed:
> "Be you my guides, with your auspicious aid,
> And lead my footsteps, till the branch be found,
> Whose glittering shadow gilds the sacred ground."
>   DRYDEN, *AEneid*, BOOK VI.

The branch was soon found, for the doves, fluttering away, yet keeping within view of AEneas, presently perched upon a tree, and from out the foliage of this tree, as the Trojan chief approached it, there flashed upon his eyes the gleam of the golden bough. Eagerly he plucked off the branch, and gladly bore it to the cave of the Sibyl.

They now set out on their perilous journey. At the mouth of the gloomy cavern by the side of Lake Avernus, which was the opening to the road that led to Hades—the kingdom of the dead—they offered sacrifices to the gods. Then they plunged into the cave, the Sibyl going first, and AEneas following with sword drawn, as his guide had directed. Many strange and terrible sights they saw on the way.

>   Full in the midst an aged elm
> Broods darkly o'er the shadowy realm;
> There dream-land phantoms rest the wing,
> Men say, and 'neath its foliage cling,
> And many monstrous shapes beside.
> There Centaurs, Scyllas, fish and maid,
> There Briareus' hundred-handed shade.
>   CONINGTON, *AEneid*, BOOK VI.

AEneas was about to rush on these monsters with his sword, when the Sibyl informed him that they were no real beings but merely phantoms. Then they came to the Styx—the river of Hades, over which the ferryman Cha'ron, grim and long-bearded, conveyed the departed spirits, in his iron-colored boat, using a pole to steer with.

> The watery passage Charon keeps
> Sole warden of these murky deeps.
>   CONINGTON, *AEneid*, BOOK VI.

No living being was permitted to enter Charon's boat, or to cross the Stygian river without the passport of the golden bough. This could be obtained only by special favor of some powerful god, and few had been so favored. Even the dead, if their bodies had not received burial rites, were refused admission to the boat, until they had wandered on the shore for a hundred years. So the Sibyl told AEneas when he inquired why some were ferried over, while others were driven back, lamenting that they were not allowed to pass to their destined abode.

> "The ghosts rejected are the unhappy crew
> Deprived of sepulchres and funeral due;
> The boatman, Charon; those, the buried host,
> He ferries over to the further coast;
> Nor dares his transport vessel cross the waves
> With such whose bones are not composed in graves.
> A hundred years they wander on the shore;
> At length, their penance done, are wafted o'er."
>   DRYDEN, *AEneid*, BOOK VI.

One of these unhappy spirits AEneas recognised as that of his pilot Palinurus, who told the hero that he had not been drowned, or plunged into the sea by a god, for he did not know of the treachery of Somnus. He had fallen overboard, he said, and kept afloat for three days, clinging to the helm, which he had dragged away with him. On the fourth day he had swam ashore on the Italian coast, and would have been out of danger, had not the cruel natives there fallen upon him with their swords. His body he said was now tossing about in the waters of the harbor of Ve'li-a, and he begged AEneas to seek it out and give it burial, or, if this was impossible, to devise some means of helping him across the Stygian river. This latter proposal the Sibyl forbade as impious, saying that the decrees of the gods could not be thus altered. But she consoled Palinurus by predicting that the people of Velia should be punished by plagues from heaven until they erected a tomb to his memory, and that the place should forever bear his name. The modern name of the place is *Capo di Palinuro*—Cape of Palinurus.

[Illustration with caption: AENEAS CROSSING THE STYX. (Drawn by Varian.)]

AEneas and his guide now approached the river. Charon at once seeing that they were mortal beings, roughly ordered them to advance no further.

> "Mortal, whate'er, who this forbidden path
> In arms presum'st to tread! I charge thee, stand,
> And tell thy name, and business in the land!
> Know, this the realm of night—the Stygian shore;

> My boat conveys no living bodies o'er."
> DRYDEN, *AEneid*, BOOK VI.

The Sibyl answered that her companion was the Trojan AEneas, illustrious for piety and valor, who desired to go down to the shades to see and converse with his father Anchises. Then from underneath her robe she produced the golden bough.

> No more was needful; for the gloomy god
> Stood mute with awe, to see the golden rod;
> Admired the destined offering to his queen—
> A venerable gift, so rarely seen.
> DRYDEN, *AEneid*, BOOK VI.

The two mortals were now received into the boat and soon ferried safely to the other side. There they saw the three-headed watchdog Cer'be-rus, who made the dreary region resound with his frightful barking. The Sibyl flung him a cake composed of honey and drugged grain, which he greedily swallowed. Then the monster fell into a deep sleep. The passage being thus free, they proceeded on their way. Soon they came to the place where the judge Mi'nos sat, examining into the lives and crimes of departed mortals.

> Minos, the strict inquisitor, appears;
> And lives and crimes, with his assessors, hears.
> Round, in his urn, the blended balls he rolls,
> Absolves the just, and dooms the guilty souls.
> DRYDEN, *AEneid*, BOOK VI.

In one of the outer regions of the shadowy world he had now entered, a region which the poet calls the "Mourning Fields," AEneas beheld the shade of the unhappy Carthaginian queen.

> Whom when the Trojan hero hardly knew,
> Obscure in shades, and with a doubtful view,
> With tears he first approached the sullen shade;
> And as his love inspired him, thus he said:
> "Unhappy queen! then is the common breath
> Of rumor true, in your reported death,
> And I, alas! the cause?—By Heaven, I vow,
> And all the powers that rule the realms below,
> Unwilling I forsook your friendly state,
> Commanded by the gods, and forced by Fate."
> DRYDEN, *AEneid*, BOOK VI.

But the mournful shade made no answer to the Trojan hero's vows and regrets.

> Disdainfully she looked; then turning round,
> She fixed her eyes unmoved upon the ground;
> And, what he says and swears, regards no more
> Than the deaf rocks, when the loud billows roar:
> But whirled away, to shun his hateful sight,
> Hid in the forest, and the shades of night:
> Then sought Sichaeus through the shady grove,
> Who answered all her cares, and equalled all her love.
>   DRYDEN, *AEneid*, BOOK VI.

They next came to the Field of Heroes, where AEneas saw the shades of many of his brave comrades of the Trojan war. The ghosts crowded round him, standing on the right hand and on the left. Nor were they satisfied with seeing him once. They wished to detain him a long time, to talk with him and learn the cause of his strange visit. But the Sibyl warned him that they must hasten forward, and presently they came to a place where the path divided itself into two. The right led by the walls of Pluto's palace to the happy Field of E-lys'ium, the land of the blessed. The left path led to Tar'ta-rus, the abode of the wicked. At this place AEneas saw a vast prison, inclosed by a triple wall, around which flowed the Phleg'e-thon, a river of fire. In front of it was a huge gate of solid adamant.

> There rolls swift Plegethon, with thund'ring sound,
> His broken rocks, and whirls his surges round.
> On mighty columns rais'd sublime are hung
> The massy gates impenetrably strong.
> In vain would men, in vain would gods essay,
> To hew the beams of adamant away.
>   PITT, *AEneid*, BOOK VI.

Deep groans and the grating of iron and the clanking of chains were heard from out these walls. None except the lost souls the Sibyl said, were allowed to pass the threshold of Tartarus, and the punishments there, and the crimes for which the wicked suffered, were such that she could not tell them though she had a hundred tongues.

> "Had I a hundred mouths, a hundred tongues,
> And throats of brass, inspired with iron lungs,
> I could not half those horrid crimes repeat,
> Nor half the punishment those crimes have met."
>   DRYDEN, *AEneid*, BOOK VI.

Some were punished by being tied to perpetually revolving wheels of fire. This was the fate of a king named Ix-i'on. Others, like the robber Sis'y-phus, were condemned to roll huge stones up a hill, and just on reaching the summit, the stones would slip from their grasp and roll to the foot of the hill, and the unhappy beings had to roll them up again, and so on forever. Others were tortured like Pi-rith'o-us, who stood under a great hanging rock, which threatened every moment to tumble down upon him, keeping him in constant terror.

The Sibyl told AEneas of these and many other punishments appointed by the gods for bad men. Then they hastened to Pluto's palace, and the hero fixed the golden bough on the door, after which, proceeding on their way, they soon came to the Elysian Fields—the abode of those who while on earth had led good and useful lives. Here were delightful green fields and shady groves; the sky was bright, the air pure and balmy. The happy spirits were engaged in sports, such as had been their pleasure when in the world above. Some were wrestling on the grassy plain, others exercising with spear and bow, others singing and dancing.

> Their airy limbs in sports they exercise,
> And, on the green, contend the wrestler's prize.
> Some, in heroic verse, divinely sing;
> Others in artful measures lead the ring.
> DRYDEN, *AEneid*, BOOK VI.

On the bank of a beautiful river—the E-rid'a-nus—flowing over sands of gold, was a band of spirits whose heads were crowned with white garlands. These were the spirits of patriots who had fought for their country, poets who had sung the praises of the gods, and men who had improved life by the invention of useful arts. In this band was Mu-sae'us, the most ancient of poets. Approaching him the Sibyl inquired where Anchises might be found. "None of us here," answered Musaeus, "has a fixed abode. We dwell in shady groves, or lie on the banks of crystal streams. But come over this eminence and I will direct you to him you seek."

Musaeus then led them to a spot from which they could view the bright Elysian fields around, and pointed to a green dale where at last they beheld Anchises. The hero hastened to approach his father, eager to embrace him, and thrice did he attempt to throw his arms about his neck, but thrice did the form escape his hold, for it was nothing but thin air.

> Thrice, around his neck, his arms he threw
> And thrice the flitting shadow slipped away,
> Like winds, or empty dreams, that fly the day.
> DRYDEN, *AEneid*, BOOK VI.

Anchises told his son much about the dwellers in Elysium. On the banks of the river Lethe—the river of forgetfulness—was a countless multitude of spirits which, he said, were yet to live in earthly bodies. They were the souls of unborn generations of men. Amongst them, he pointed out to AEneas, the spirits of many of those who were to be his own descendants in the kingdom he was to establish in Italy.

> The father-spirit leads
> The priestess and his son through swarms of shades,
> And takes a rising ground, from thence to see
> The long procession of his progeny.
> DRYDEN, *AEneid*, BOOK VI.

From this rising ground AEneas saw the shadowy forms of future heroes of Rome—of Rom'u-lus, who was to found the city—of Brutus, Ca-mil'lus, Fa'bi-us, and of the mighty Caesars.

> "Lo! Caesar there and all his seed,
> Iulus' progeny decreed
>   To pass 'neath heaven's high dome.
> This, this is he, so oft the theme
> Of your prophetic fancy's dream,
>   Augustus Caesar, Jove's own strain."
> CONINGTON, *AEneid*, BOOK VI.

Anchises next told AEneas of the wars he should have to wage, and instructed him how to avoid or overcome every difficulty. Then he conducted his visitors to the gates of Sleep, through which the gods of Hades sent dreams to the upper world—true dreams through the gate of horn, and false dreams through the gate of ivory. Here Anchises left them. Then departing by the ivory gate from the kingdom of the dead, they returned to the Cumaean cave, and AEneas forthwith proceeded to his ships.

> Sleep gives his name to portals twain;
>   One all of horn, they say,
> Through which authentic spectres gain
>   Quick exit into day,
> And one which bright with ivory gleams,
> Whence Pluto sends delusive dreams.
> Conversing still, the sire attends
>   The travellers on their road,
> And through the ivory portal sends
>   From forth the unseen abode.
> The chief betakes him to the fleet,
> Well pleased again his crew to meet.
> CONINGTON, *AEneid*, BOOK VI.

VI. AENEAS ARRIVES IN LATIUM—WELCOMED BY KING LATINUS.

The object of his visit to the Sibyl being accomplished, the Trojan chief set sail and steered along the coast in the direction of the promised land. But soon again he had occasion to put ashore. His nurse, Ca-i-e'ta, having died shortly after the departure of the fleet from Cumae, he desired to give funeral honors to her remains. This duty performed, he named the place (modern Gaeta) in memory of his faithful and attached old servant.

> And thou, O matron of immortal fame!
> Here dying, to the shore hast left thy name;
> Gaieta still the place is called from thee,
> The nurse of great AEneas' infancy.
> Here rest thy bones in rich Hesperia's plains;
> Thy name ('tis all a ghost can have) remains.
>   DRYDEN, *AEneid*, BOOK VII.

Again resuming their voyage they came near an island where dwelt the sorceress, Cir'ce, who by her enchantments changed men into beasts. As they passed the island the Trojans heard with horror the roaring of lions and the howling of wolves, once human beings, but transformed by the cruel goddess into the shape of those savage animals. Aided, however, by favorable winds sent by the friendly Neptune, they sped away from this dangerous spot, and soon they were near the end of their wanderings. At the dawn of next morning they beheld a spacious grove, through which a pleasant river, tinted with the hue of the yellow sand, burst forth into the sea. This was the Tiber on whose banks in the distant future was to be founded the city in which the descendants of the Trojan prince should hold imperial sway. AEneas, though not aware that he was so close to the destined spot, commanded his pilots to turn the ships towards the land, and joyfully they entered the river. All around, the Trojan chief, as he gazed upon the scene, could hear the sweet music of the groves.

> Embowered amid the silvan scene
> Old Tiber winds his banks between,
> Around, gay birds of diverse wing,
> Accustomed there to fly or sing,
> Were fluttering on from spray to spray
> And soothing ether with their lay.
>   CONINGTON, *AEneid*, BOOK VII.

The country in which the Trojans had now landed was called Latium, and La-ti'nus was its king. Like most great kings of ancient times, he was descended from a god. His father, Faunus, was the grandson of Saturn, the predecessor and father of Jupiter.

Latinus was advanced in years, and he had no male heir, but he had an only daughter, young and beautiful, whose name was La-vin'i-a. Many of the princes of the neighboring states eagerly sought Lavinia's hand in marriage. Chief amongst them was Turnus, king of the Ru'tu-li, a brave and handsome youth. Lavinia's mother, Queen A-ma'ta, favored the suit of Turnus, and desired to have him as her son-in-law.

But the gods had not willed it so, and they sent signs from heaven— signs of their disapproval of the proposed union. In the inner court of the palace of Latinus stood a laurel tree which had been preserved for many years with great reverence. From this tree, it was said, Latinus had given the name Lau-ren'tines to the inhabitants of the country. Just about the time the Trojan fleet was entering the Tiber an immense number of bees were seen to cluster on the top of the laurel tree, and soon linking together, feet to feet, they swung in a strange manner from one of the boughs. The king's soothsayer explained this to mean that a foreign hero was then coming into the country, and that he would one day be its ruler.

About the same time, while the princess Lavinia was bringing fire to an altar where her father stood preparing to offer sacrifice, the flame seemed to catch her flowing hair, and to envelop her whole body in its glowing light, without, however, inflicting the slightest injury. The soothsayer declared that this was a sign that Lavinia would be great and famous, but that through her war should come on the people.

> "The nymph who scatters flaming fires around,
> Shall shine with honor, shall herself be crowned;
> But, caused by her irrevocable fate,
> War shall the country waste, and change the state."
> DRYDEN, *AEneid*, BOOK VII.

The king was much troubled by these events and so he went into the wood, to the tomb of his father, Faunus, by whom answers were given in dreams to those who, having offered sacrifices, lay down and slept under the trees. Latinus, after performing the necessary ceremonies, soon heard the voice of his father warning him not to give his daughter in marriage to any prince of his own country. "A foreigner," said he, "is coming who shall be your son-in-law, and his descendants shall exalt our name to the stars. From his race, united with ours, shall spring mighty men, who shall conquer and rule the world to its farthest limits."

King Latinus did not conceal his dream. On the contrary he proclaimed it aloud to his people. And so the news of the arrival of the strangers with their ships came not as a surprise to the inhabitants of Latium.

Meanwhile the Trojans having landed upon the Latian coast, Aeneas and several of his chiefs, accompanied by his son Iulus, sat down under a tall tree to refresh themselves with food and drink. They had cakes of wheat, the last of their store, spread upon the grass, and upon these cakes they placed wild fruits which they had gathered in the woods. When they had eaten the fruit, they proceeded to eat the cakes, upon which Iulus exclaimed, "What, are we eating our tables too?" The boy had no thought of the meaning of what they had been doing. But Aeneas joyfully recognized it as the fulfillment of the threatening prophecy of the Harpy Celaena. The cakes were the tables, and the Trojans had now eaten them without harm.

Then Aeneas spoke encouraging words to his companions. "Hail, O land, destined to us by the Fates! This is our home; this is our country. For my father too (as I now remember), told me in Elysium these same secrets, saying: 'When hunger shall compel you, my son, wafted to an unknown shore, to eat up your tables, your provisions having failed, then you may hope for a settlement after your toils, and in that place you may found your first city.' Here was that famine of which he spoke. Our calamities are now at an end. Let us, then, with the first light of to-morrow's sun, explore this country, ascertain who are its inhabitants, and where their cities are."

Next day, when Aeneas learned what country he was in, and the name of its king, he sent ambassadors—a hundred of his chiefs—to wait on Latinus and beg his friendship and assistance, furnishing them with costly gifts for the king. The chiefs hastened on their mission to Latinus, and Aeneas meanwhile began to mark out the boundaries of a new city.

When the Trojan ambassadors reached Lau-ren-tum, the capital of Latium, they were admitted to the royal palace and brought into the presence of the king, who was seated on his throne—a magnificent structure raised aloft on a hundred columns, around which were numerous statues of the king's ancestors, carved in cedar wood. Latinus, after civilly greeting the strangers, bade them say for what purpose they had come to Italy; whether they had landed in his country because of having missed their course at sea, or through stress of weather. He added that whatever was the object of their coming, they should receive kind treatment from him and his people.

To these friendly words Ilioneus, speaking for the Trojans, replied that it was no storm that sent them to Italy. "Willingly and with design," said he, "have we come to your shores, O king, after having been expelled from a kingdom once the most powerful under the sun. Our race is derived from Jupiter himself, and our chief, Aeneas, descended from the gods, has sent us to your court. All the world has heard of the destruction of our city, Troy. Driven by misfortunes over many seas, we beg for a settlement in your country. Dardanus, our ancestor, was born in this land, and now his descendants, directed by the gods, come to the home of their father." They then presented to the king the costly gifts which Aeneas had sent.

> "Our prince presents with his request,
> Some small remains of what his sire possessed;
> This golden charger, snatched from burning Troy,
> Anchises did in sacrifice employ;
> This royal robe and this tiara wore
> Old Priam, and this golden sceptre bore
> In full assemblies, and in solemn games;
> These purple vests were weaved by Dardan dames."
> DRYDEN, *AEneid*, BOOK VII.

After Ilioneus had ceased speaking, the king was silent for some time, pondering on the words of his father which he had heard in the dream. Aeneas, he thought, must be the foreigner, destined to be his son-in-law, whose descendants should rule the world. Then he addressed the Trojans, saying that what they asked should gladly be given, and requesting them to tell their chief, Aeneas, to visit him. "Bear this message too," said he, "from me to your king. I have a daughter whom the gods do not permit me to give in marriage to any of our own nation. There is a prediction that my son-in-law shall be a stranger, and that his race shall exalt our name to the stars. I judge that your chief is the man thus destined by the fates, and this too is my own wish."

Then Latinus gave valuable presents to the Trojans—to each a steed from the royal stables, with rich purple trappings. To Aeneas himself he sent a chariot and a pair of horses of the breed which the sorceress, Circe, had obtained from the sun-god, her father. With these presents, the Trojan ambassadors, mounted on their splendid steeds, returned to their chief, and joyfully informed him of the king's message and invitation.

But this friendship shown to the Trojans by King Latinus was not at all agreeable to Juno. On the contrary that unforgiving goddess was filled with grief and anger when she saw Aeneas and his people engaged in building their city and settling themselves in their new home, and so she resolved to stir up strife between the Trojans and Latinus. With this object she called to her aid A-lec'to, one of the three terrible sisters called Furies. These were evil deities whose usual occupation was to scourge and torment condemned souls in the kingdom of Pluto, and drive them to the gates of Tartarus. They sometimes also caused trouble in the upper world, by exciting dissensions and bringing about wars. This was the service which Juno now required, and so, addressing Alecto she requested her to stir up discord between the people of Latium and the followers of Aeneas.

> "'Tis thine to ruin realms, o'erturn a state,
> Betwixt the dearest friends to raise debate,
> And kindle kindred blood to mutual hate.

> Thy hand o'er towns the funeral torch displays,
> And forms a thousand ills ten thousand ways.
> Now, shake from out thy frightful breast, the seeds
> Of envy, discord, and of cruel deeds;
> Confound the peace established, and prepare
> Their souls to hatred, and their hands to war."
> DRYDEN, *AEneid*, BOOK VII.

Alecto, glad to be thus employed, hastened to the palace of Latinus, and sought out Queen Amata, who, as has already been said, desired to have Turnus for her son-in-law. The Furies were hideous beings in appearance, for instead of hair they had serpents coiled around their heads. Alecto unseen by Amata, shook her terrible locks, upon which one of the reptiles darted into the dress of the queen; and, gliding unfelt around her body, infused into her heart a violent hatred of the Trojans.

> Unseen, unfelt, the fiery serpent skims,
> His baneful breath inspiring as he glides;
> Now like a chain around her neck he rides;
> Now like a fillet to her head repairs,
> And with his circling volumes folds her hairs.
> At first the silent venom slid with ease,
> And seized her cooler senses by degrees.
> DRYDEN, *AEneid*, BOOK VII.

Amata now endeavored to turn the mind of Latinus against the proposed marriage, but he was not to be moved from his purpose of forming an alliance with the Trojans. Then the queen filled with anger rushed out of the palace, as if in a frenzy, and hastening through the city called upon the women of Latium to espouse her cause and the cause of their country. She also carried off her daughter, and concealed her in the mountains, to prevent her marriage with the hated Trojan.

Having thus kindled discord in the family of Latinus, Alecto next proceeded to Ar'de-a the Rutulian capital. Here she assumed the form of Cal'y-be, an aged priestess of Juno's temple, and appearing to King Turnus in a dream as he lay asleep in his palace, urged him to take up arms against Latinus and the strangers. Turnus was not yet disposed to take this course, and so he replied to the seeming priestess, that her duty was to guard the statues and temples of the gods, and he advised her to leave to men the management of affairs of peace and war. Enraged by the words of Turnus Alecto now resumed her Fury's form.

> Her eyes grow stiffened, and with sulphur burn;
> Her hideous looks, and hellish form return;
> Her curling snakes with hissings fill the place,

> And open all the furies of her face;
> Then, darting fire from her malignant eyes,
> She cast him backward as he strove to rise.
> DRYDEN, *AEneid*, BOOK VII.

Then crying out that she came from the abode of the dire sisters, and that wars and death were in her hands, she flung a fire-brand at the king, and disappeared. Turnus started from his sleep, in terror, and now his breast was filled with eager desire for war. Immediately he sent orders amongst his chiefs to prepare to defend Italy and expel the foreigners, declaring that he and his people were a match for Trojans and Latins combined.

Meanwhile Alecto, her mission of discord not yet completed, appeared among a band of Trojan youths who with Iulus at their head were amusing themselves by hunting in the forest. The Fury hurled a fire-brand at the hounds, and suddenly, as if seized with madness, they rushed in pursuit of a beautiful young stag which was sporting among the trees. This stag was a pet of Syl'vi-a, the daughter of Tyr'rheus, one of the herdsmen of King Latinus. Iulus seeing the hounds in pursuit, followed them, and shot at and wounded the stag. The animal fled to the house of Tyrrheus, where Sylvia, seeing her pet covered with blood, broke out into loud lamentations. Her father in a fit of anger seized a weapon, and joined by some of his friends rushed upon Iulus and his companions. The alarm quickly reaching the camp of the Trojans several of them hastened to assist their countrymen, and a fierce battle ensued, in which many of the Latians or Latins were killed. Thus the evil project of Juno was accomplished.

> Then Juno thus: "The grateful work is done,
> The seeds of discord sowed, the war begun;
> Frauds, fears and fury, have possessed the state,
> And fixed the causes of a lasting hate."
> DRYDEN, *AEneid*, BOOK VII.

And now the Latian youth, chiefly shepherds, who had taken part with Tyrrheus, rushed from the field of battle into the city, carrying with them the bodies of their friends who had been slain, and crying to the gods and to King Latinus for vengeance upon the Trojans. Just then King Turnus appeared with a force of his Rutulians, and addressed the people in words which excited them to the highest pitch of fury. He told them that foreigners had been invited to rule in their country, and that the chief of the intruders was to have the princess who had been promised to him to be his wife.

Then a great multitude of Latians and Rutulians hastened to the palace of King Latinus, and demanded that he should at once declare war against the Trojans. Latinus refused to do what he knew was against the decrees of the gods, and he warned the people that evil would come upon them if they persevered in their mad opposition to the will of heaven. He also warned Turnus that he would be punished for inciting such a war, and that he should one day seek the aid of the gods, and seek it in vain. As for himself, he said, he was an old man. Their folly could deprive him only of a happy ending of a life which could not be much further prolonged. He then retired to his palace, and gave up the reins of government, leaving the people to pursue their own course.

> He said no more, but, in his walls confined,
> Shut out the woes which he too well divined;
> Nor with the rising storm would vainly strive,
> But left the helm, and let the vessel drive.
> DRYDEN, *AEneid*, BOOK VII.

In spite of the warning of their king, the Latians now resolved upon war against the Trojans and they demanded that the gates of the temple of Janus should be thrown open. Janus was the most ancient king who reigned in Italy. When he died he was worshipped as a god, and a magnificent temple was erected in his honor. The gates of this temple were always open in times of war and shut in times of peace. They were opened by the king, and in later ages, when Rome was a republic, the president or consul performed the ceremony dressed in robes of purple and attended by multitudes of citizens and soldiers, with the blaring of trumpets.

> Two gates of steel (the name of Mars they bear,
> And still are worshipped with religious fear)
> Before his temple stand; the dire abode,
> And the feared issues of the furious god,
> Then, when the sacred senate votes the wars,
> The Roman consul their decree declares,
> And in his robes the sounding gates unbars.
> The youth in military shouts arise,
> And the loud trumpets break the yielding skies.
> DRYDEN, *AEneid*, BOOK Vii.

The Latians now requested their king to unlock the gates of the temple of Janus in accordance with the ancient custom. Latinus refused saying that to do so would be a defiance of the gods. But the goddess Juno, resolved that there should be no peace, descended from the skies, and with her own hands pushed back the bolts of brass, and flung wide open the gates. Then the cry of war went forth throughout the land and everywhere men began to prepare for the conflict, giving up their work in the fields to get ready their spears and shields and battle-axes. Soon a vast number of warriors was marshalled under King Turnus to drive the Trojans out of Italy. Vergil gives a long list of the famous chiefs who assembled on this occasion.

First came Me-zen'ti-us, an Etrurian king, fierce in war, but a despiser of the gods. His own people had expelled him from their country, for his cruelty, and he had taken refuge with King Turnus. His son Lausus also came to the war with a thousand men from the Etrurian city of A-gyl'la. Next came the brave Av-en-ti'nus, son of the renowned hero, Her'cu-les, who performed those marvelous feats, of which we read with wonder in the ancient legends. Aventinus was a warrior of terrible appearance, his body covered with the shaggy hide of an enormous lion, the white tusks displayed above his head.

King Caec'u-lus, son of the god Vulcan, came from the city of Prae-nes'te with an army who fought with slings, wore helmets of wolf-skins, and marched with one foot naked.

> Nor arms they wear, nor swords and bucklers wield,
> Nor drive the chariot through the dusty field;
> But whirl from leathern slings huge balls of lead;
> And spoils of yellow wolves adorn their head;
> The left foot naked, when they march to fight;
> But in a bull's raw hide they sheath the right.
> DRYDEN, *AEneid*, BOOK VII.

From the mountains of Etruria came the gallant horseman, Mes-sa'pus, Neptune's son, "whom none had power to prostrate by fire or steel." The mighty King Clausus led to the field a great host from the country of the Sabines, and an army of the Qui-ri'tes from the town of Cu'res. This name, Quirites was in later ages one of the names by which the citizens of Rome were called. Another of the warriors was Umbro, chief of the Maru'vi-i, who could charm serpents and heal wounds inflicted by their bites.

[Illustration with caption: CAMILLA. (Drawn by Varian.)]

All these and many more of the princes of Italy, assembled with their armies at the call of Turnus. Greatest amongst them was Turnus himself, tallest by a head, and clad in armor brilliant with embroidered gold. There was one female warrior amongst his allies. This was Ca-mil'la, the queen of the Volscians. She was the daughter of King Met'a-bus, who, like Mezentius, had been driven from his kingdom by his own people, because he was a cruel tyrant. In his flight, for the enraged people pursued him to take his life, he carried with him his infant daughter Camilla. Coming to the bank of a river and still pursued by his enemies, he bound the child fast to his javelin, and holding the weapon in his hands, he prayed to Di-a'na, goddess of hunters and hunting, and dedicated his daughter to her saying,

"To thee, goddess of the woods, I devote this child to be thy handmaid, and committing her to the wind, I implore thee to receive her as thine own." Then he hurled the spear across the river, and plunging into the water swam to the other side, where he found the javelin fixed in the bank, and the infant uninjured.

After this achievement Metabus retired to the mountains, where he led the life of a shepherd. As soon as the child was able to hold a weapon in her hand, he trained her to the use of javelins and arrows and she grew up to be a brave and skillful warrior. In course of time she returned to the kingdom from which her father had been expelled, and became celebrated as a runner of wondrous speed.

VII. ALLIANCE WITH EVANDER—VULCAN MAKES ARMS FOR AENEAS—THE FAMOUS SHIELD.

Meanwhile AEneas was considering how to defend himself and his people against the enemy who was thus marshalling such mighty forces against him. He thought of many plans without being able to decide upon any.

> This way, and that, he turns his anxious mind;
> Thinks, and rejects the counsels he designed;
> Explores himself in vain in every part,
> And gives no rest to his distracted heart
> DRYDEN, *AEneid*, BOOK VIII.

But fortune again favored the pious chief. In a dream the river god, Tib-e-ri'nus, arrayed in garb of green, with a crown of reeds upon his head (old Father Tiber himself, the guardian genius of Rome in later ages) appeared to him, and told him where to seek help. He repeated the prophecy of Helenus, about the sow with her litter of thirty young, and he directed AEneas to repair to Pal-lan-te'um, a city further up the river, whose king, E-van'der, being frequently at war with the Latians, would gladly join the Trojans. The good father promised that he himself would conduct the Trojans along his banks, and bear them safely on his waters until they reached the Kingdom of Evander.

> "To thy free passage I submit my streams.
> Wake, son of Venus, from thy pleasing dreams!
> And when the setting stars are lost in day,
> To Juno's power thy just devotion pay;
> With sacrifice the wrathful queen appease;
> Her pride at length shall fall, her fury cease.
> When thou return'st victorious from the war,
> Perform thy vows to me with grateful care.
> The god am I, whose yellow water flows
> Around these fields, and fattens as it goes;
> Tiber my name—among the rolling floods
> Renowned on earth, esteemed among the gods."
> DRYDEN, *AEneid*, BOOK VIII.

Old Father Tiber then plunged into the middle of the river, and disappeared from the hero's view. When AEneas awoke he immediately prepared for his journey, selecting two ships from his fleet and furnishing them with men and arms. As he was about to depart, the prophecy only just repeated by the river god was fulfilled before his eyes; for on the bank where he stood, a white sow suddenly appeared with a litter of thirty young ones.

> When lo! a sudden prodigy;
>   A milk-white sow is seen
> Stretched with her young ones, white as she,
>   Along the margent green.
> AEneas takes them, dam and brood,
> And o'er the altars pours their blood,
> To thee, great Juno, e'en to thee,
>   High heaven's majestic queen.
>   CONINGTON, *AEneid*, BOOK VIII.

AEneas then started on his voyage, Father Tiber making the passage easy by calming his turbid river so that its surface was as smooth as a peaceful lake. At noon next day the Trojans came in sight of Pallanteum, and soon afterwards they turned their ships toward the land, and approached the city. Just then King Evander, accompanied by his son Pallas and many of his chiefs, was offering a sacrifice to Hercules in a grove outside the city walls. Alarmed at the sudden appearance of the vessels, they made a movement as if to depart in haste from their altars. But Pallas forbade them to interrupt the sacred rites, and advancing to meet the strangers, he addressed them from a rising ground, asking who they were, and for what purpose they had come. AEneas, speaking from the deck of one of his ships, and holding in his hand an olive branch, the emblem of peace, replied, saying, "You see before you sons of Troy, and enemies of the Latians, who have declared war against us. We seek King Evander. Bear him these tidings, and say to him that we have come asking for his alliance in arms."

Astonished at hearing that the visitors were the illustrious Trojans whose fame had already spread throughout the world, Pallas invited them to land and come as guests to his father's house. AEneas gladly accepted the invitation, and the young prince conducted them to the grove, and introduced them to King Evander. This Evander was by birth a Greek. He had come from the Grecian province of Ar-ca'di-a, and the city he founded in Italy he called after the name of his native Arcadian city of Pallanteum. AEneas, however, had no fear that Evander, though a Greek, would be an enemy of his, for they were both of the same blood, being both descended from Atlas, the mighty hero who of old supported the heavens on his shoulders. Mercury, the father of Evander, was the son of Ma'i-a, a daughter of Atlas; and Dardanus, the founder of Troy, and ancestor of its kings, was son of E-lec'tra, another daughter of Atlas. AEneas reminded

Evander of this relationship and reminded him also that the Rutulians and Latians were enemies of Evander and his people, as well as of the Trojans.

"They are the nation," said he, "which pursue you with cruel war, and they think that if they expel us from the country, nothing can hinder them from reducing all Italy under their yoke. Let us therefore form an alliance against this common foe. We Trojans have amongst us men stout of heart in battle and experienced in war."

While the hero was speaking, the king kept his eyes intently fixed upon him, for in his face and figure he saw the resemblance of the great Anchises, whom he had known in past years. Then replying to AEneas, he said, "Great chief of the Trojan race, I gladly receive and recognize you. I well recollect the words, the voice, and the features of your father, Anchises. For I remember that Priam on his way to visit his sister Hesione in Greece, also visited my country, Arcadia. Many of the Trojan princes accompanied him; but the most majestic of them all was Anchises. Much did I admire him, and I took him with me to our Arcadian city Phe'neus. At his departure he gave me costly presents, a quiver filled with Lycian arrows, a mantle interwoven with gold and two golden bridles." Evander concluded by consenting to the proposal of AEneas for an alliance against the Latians—

> "The league you ask, I offer as your right;
> And when to-morrow's sun reveals the light,
> With swift supplies you shall be sent away."
> DRYDEN, *AEneid*, BOOK VIII.

The Trojans were now hospitably entertained by King Evander. Seated on the greensward, they partook of a plenteous repast, and when the banquet was over, the king explained to AEneas and his companions the meaning of the religious festivities in which they had been engaged. It was through no vain superstition, he said, that they performed these solemn rites, but to commemorate their deliverance from a terrible scourge, and to give honor to their deliverer.

Then Evander related the story of the monster Ca'cus, who in former times, dwelt in a cave underneath the hill on which Pallanteum was now built. He was a giant, of enormous size and hideous to behold, for from his father Vulcan, the god of fire, he had got the power of breathing smoke and flame through his mouth and nostrils. He was a scourge and a terror to the country round, as besides being a robber, he killed and devoured men. But by good fortune the hero Hercules happened to pass that way, driving before him a herd of cattle which he had taken from another cruel monster—the three-bodied giant Ge'ry-on, whom he had destroyed. As these cattle were grazing by the river, Hercules having lain down on the bank to rest, Cacus stole four bulls and four heifers, the finest of the herd. To conceal the theft he dragged the animals backwards by the tails into his den, so that their footprints seemed to show that they had gone from the cave instead of into it. This trick had almost succeeded, for Hercules, after searching in vain for the missing animals, was about to resume his journey, when a lowing from within the cave reached his ears.

> The oxen at departing fill
> With noisy utterance grove and hill,
>   And breathe a farewell low;
> When hark! a heifer from the den
> Makes answer to the sound again
>   And mocks her wily foe.
>   CONINGTON, *AEneid*, BOOK VIII.

Hercules now knowing what had become of his cattle rushed to the top of the mount where he had seen the giant, but Cacus fled into his cave, and instantly let drop the huge stone which he kept suspended by iron chains over the entrance. This stone even the mighty Hercules could not move from its place, for it was held fast by great bolts on the inside. But searching around the mount for another entrance, he saw a rock overhanging the river, which formed a back for the cavern. Exerting his full strength, the hero wrenched this rock from its fastenings, and hurled it into the water. In the interior of the den, thus laid open, Hercules soon caught sight of the robber, and commenced to assail him with arrows and stones. Then the monster belched forth volumes of smoke and flame, concealing himself in a cloud of pitchy vapor. But Hercules now thoroughly enraged, rushed furiously into the den, and seizing Cacus by the throat, choked him to death. Great was the joy of the people when they heard of the destruction of the monster, and anniversary festivals had been held there ever since in honor of the deliverer.

After King Evander had told this story, choirs of young and old men, the priests called Sa'li-i, sang songs about the great deeds of Hercules; how when a child in his cradle he had strangled the two serpents sent by Juno to destroy him, how he had slain the furious lion of Nemea, dragged from Pluto's realms the three-headed dog Cerberus, and performed numerous other difficult and dangerous feats.

Evander and his people now returned to the city, accompanied by their Trojan guests. The king walked by the side of AEneas, and told him many things about the traditions of the place, and its early history. At one time, he said, the country had been ruled by Saturn, who, driven from the throne of the heavens by his son Jupiter, had come to Italy, and finding on the banks of the river a race of uncivilized men, had formed them into a settled society. He taught them how to till the ground, and introduced laws amongst them, and so peaceful and happy were they under his reign, that it was called the Golden Age. One of the kings long after Saturn's reign was Tiberinus, whose name was given to the river, and who became its guardian god.

The king then escorted AEneas through the town, pointing out to him many places, destined to be famous in later history, for on that very ground Romulus built his city, and Pallanteum became the celebrated Palatine Mount, one of the seven hills of Rome. When they reached the royal palace, which was not as large or magnificent as palaces often are, the king took pride in mentioning that the great Hercules, honored in life, and after death worshipped as a god, had not disdained to accept hospitality under its roof.

> He spoke, and through the narrow door
>   The great AEneas led,
> And heaped a couch upon the floor
>   With leaves and bear-skin spread.
>   CONINGTON, *AEneid*, BOOK VIII.

While the Trojan chief was being entertained by King Evander, his mother Venus was much troubled in mind thinking of the danger which threatened her son in his new settlement. She resolved that he should have all the aid in her power to supply, and so she requested Vulcan to make him a suit of armor. Vulcan was the god of smiths as well as of fire, and Venus thus appealed to him in behalf of her son.

"While the Greeks were laboring to bring destruction on Troy," said she to the fire god, who was also the god of smiths, "I did not ask your help, knowing that the ruin of the city had been decreed by the gods. But now AEneas has settled in Italy by Jupiter's command; therefore, I beg your assistance. What I wish is that you should make arms and armor for my son. Many nations have combined against him, and are sharpening their swords for the destruction of himself and his people."

Vulcan readily agreed to comply with the request of Venus. Being a god he could make arms and armor against which the power of mortal men would be of no avail. His forges, and furnaces, and anvils were in vast caves under one of the Lip'a-re isles and under Mount AEtna, and the giant Cyclops were his workmen.

> Sacred to Vulcan's name, an isle there lay,
> Betwixt Sicilia's coasts and Lipare,
> Raised high on smoking rocks; and, deep below,
> In hollow caves the fires of AEtna glow.
> The Cyclops here their heavy hammers deal;

> Loud strokes, and hissing of tormented steel,
> Are heard around; the boiling waters roar;
> And smoky flames through fuming tunnels soar.
> 		DRYDEN, *AEneid*, BOOK VIII.

To these workshops Vulcan forthwith repaired to give orders for the arms which Venus requested for her son. He found his men industriously at work making wonderful things for the gods. Some were forging a thunderbolt for Jupiter, the rays or shafts of which were of hail and watery cloud, and glaring fire and the winged wind. Others were making a war chariot for Mars, and others a shield for Minerva, ornamented with serpent's scales of gold. When Vulcan entered, he bade them lay aside all those tasks.

> "My sons! (said Vulcan), set your tasks aside;
> Your strength and master skill must now be tried.
> Arms for a hero forge—arms that require
> Your force, your speed, and all your forming fire."
> 		DRYDEN, *AEneid*, BOOK VIII.

Instantly the Cyclops set to work on their new task, and very soon rivulets of molten gold and copper and iron were flowing in flaming furnaces. A splendid shield was made, which was a sufficient defense in itself against all the weapons of King Turnus. Other things necessary for war were also put in shape, and so the work of forging arms for the Trojan hero was vigorously prosecuted.

Meantime AEneas himself, after his night's repose in the palace of Evander, was talking with the king and his son on the business which had brought him to Pallanteum. The good will of Evander was greater than his means, for his country was small, and on one side of it was the territory of his enemies, the Rutulians. He was not able, therefore, to do much for AEneas, but he knew where ample aid could be obtained. "In the neighboring state of Etruria, and not far from this spot," said he, "stands the ancient city of Agylla, founded by a nation illustrious in war—Mezentius was recently its king, a cruel and wicked man. The people, indignant at his crimes, took up arms against him and set fire to his palace. He himself fled for protection to King Turnus, with whom he now is. The Etrurians therefore have resolved to make war upon Turnus, and their ships and men are already assembled. You, AEneas, must be the leader of these people, for a soothsayer has told them that no native of Italy is destined to subdue the Rutulians, and that they must choose a foreigner to be their commander in the war. They have invited me to lead them, but I am too old to undertake such a task. I would have sent them my son, but being born of an Italian mother, he is of the people of this land. You, however, gallant leader of the Trojans, being in the prime of life, and of foreign race, are destined by the gods for this work. My son Pallas too shall take part in the expedition, and I will give him two hundred horsemen, and as many more he shall add in his own name."

Evander had scarcely ceased speaking when lightning flashed through the heavens and peals of thunder were heard and sounds as of trumpets blaring, and then across the sky were seen arms blazing brilliantly as the sun—arms such as heroes bore in battle, and they clashed with a loud resounding noise.

> Gazing up, repeated peals they hear;
> And, in a heaven serene, refulgent arms appear
> Reddening the skies, and glittering all around,
> The tempered metals clash, and yield a silver sound.
> DRYDEN, *AEneid*, BOOK VIII.

AEneas understood this marvelous apparition, and he explained it to his astonished companions as a call to him from heaven. His divine mother, he said, had told him that she would send that sign, and that she would bring him arms made by Vulcan. Then he offered the usual sacrifices to the gods, after which he went to his ships, and chose from his followers some to accompany him to Agylla, directing the others to return to the camp at Laurentum, and inform Iulus of the progress of their affairs at Pallanteum. Preparations for departure were now made. Evander gave AEneas horses for himself and his companions, and when all was ready, the king affectionately embraced his son, and bade him a tender farewell, praying to the gods that he might live to see him come back in safety.

The Trojan chief and his warriors, among whom were the faithful Achates and Pallas at the head of his four hundred horsemen, then set forth from the city, amid the acclamations of the people. They soon came within sight of the camp of the Etrurians, who, under the command of one of their chiefs named Tarchon, had pitched their tents on a wide plain not many miles from Pallanteum.

But before joining his new allies, AEneas had a meeting with his goddess mother. Down from the clouds she came, beautiful as the sun, bearing with her the arms that Vulcan had made, and seeing her son alone on the bank of a small stream, in a secluded vale, to which he had retired for a brief rest, she presented herself before him. At his feet she placed the gifts she had promised, telling him that now he might not fear to meet his foes in battle.

> "Behold! (she said) performed in every part,
> My promise made, and Vulcan's labored art.
> Now seek, secure, the Latian enemy.

And haughty Turnus to the field defy."
    DRYDEN, *AEneid*, BOOK VIII.

Beautiful arms and armor they were, such as could be designed and fashioned only by a god—a sword and a spear, and a helmet with a blazing crest, and a breastplate of flaming bronze, and greaves of gold and electrum. But most wonderful of all was the shield, upon which were depicted the glories and triumphs in later ages of the mighty men of Rome, the descendants of Iulus, for Vulcan, being a god, had the gift of seeing into futurity.

> There, embossed, the heavenly smith had wrought
> (Not in the rolls of future fate untaught)
> The wars in order; and the race divine
> Of warriors issuing from the Julian line.
>   DRYDEN, *AEneid*, BOOK VIII.

[Illustration: AENEAS WITH HIS WONDERFUL ARMOR. (Drawn by Varian.)]

Vergil's description of this prophetic shield occupies the concluding portion of the eighth book of the AEneid. It is a summary of notable events in the history of Rome from the time of Romulus, who founded the city, to the time of the Emperor Augustus. The achievements of Augustus are particularly dwelt on, for he was the friend and patron of the poet, and Vergil, therefore, gave special prominence to the part taken by him in the extension of the great empire. At the famous sea-battle of Ac'ti-um (B.C. 31) near the promontory of Leu-ca'te in Greece, Augustus, aided by A-grip'pa, defeated the forces of Antony and the celebrated Egyptian Queen Cle-o-pa'tra, and this victory made him master of the Roman world. On the shield of AEneas the fight at Actium was shown on a sea of molten gold, in the midst of which were represented the fleets of ships with their brazen prows.

> Betwixt the quarters, flows a golden sea;
> But foaming surges there in silver play.
> The dancing dolphins with their tails divide
> The glittering waves, and cut the precious tide.
> Amid the main, two mighty fleets engage;
> Their brazen beaks opposed with equal rage,
> Actium surveys the well-disputed prize;
> Leucate's watery plain with foamy billows fries.
> Young Caesar, on the stern in armor bright,
> Here leads the Romans and their gods to fight;
> Agrippa seconds him, with prosperous gales,
> And, with propitious gods, his foes assails.

> A naval crown, that binds his manly brows,
> The happy fortune of the fight foreshows.
>   DRYDEN, *AEneid*, BOOK VIII.

On another part of the shield were shown scenes of the Emperor's three days' Triumph in Rome after his great conquest—the procession of vanquished nations, the games and the sacrifices to the gods, and Augustus himself seated on a throne in front of the temple of Apollo.

> The victor to the gods his thanks expressed;
> And Rome triumphant with his presence blessed.
> Three hundred temples in the town he placed;
> With spoils and altars every temple graced.
> Three shining nights and three succeeding days,
> The fields resound with shouts, the streets with praise.
> Great Caesar sits sublime upon his throne,
> Before Apollo's porch of Parian stone;
> Accepts the presents vowed for victory;
> And hangs the monumental crowns on high.
> Vast crowds of vanquished nations march along,
> Various in arms, in habit, and in tongue.
>   DRYDEN, *AEneid*, BOOK VIII.

AEneas viewed these scenes with wonder and delight, though ignorant of what they meant, and putting on the beautiful armor, he bore upon his shoulder the fortunes of his descendants.

> These figures, on the shield divinely wrought,
> By Vulcan labored, and by Venus brought,
> With joy and wonder fill the hero's thought.
> Unknown the names, he yet admires the grace;
> And bears aloft the fame and fortune of his race.
>   DRYDEN, *AEneid*, BOOK VIII.

Vergil's description of the shield of AEneas is in imitation of Homer's beautiful description in the Iliad of the shield of Achilles, also made by Vulcan.

VIII. TURNUS ATTACKS THE TROJAN CAMP—NISUS AND EURYALUS.

Arrayed in his new and splendid armor, the Trojan chief rejoined his companions, and then proceeded to the Etrurian camp, where he formed a league with Tarchon. Meanwhile his enemies were not inactive, for Juno sent Iris down from heaven to the Rutulian king to urge him to bestir himself against the Trojans. "Time has brought about in your favor, O Turnus," said the messenger of Juno, "what even the gods did not dare to promise. AEneas, having left his friends and his fleet has gone to gather forces against you in the city of Evander and in Etruria. Now is your opportunity. Why do you hesitate to take advantage of it? Delay no longer, but seize the camp of the Trojans, while their leader is absent." Turnus recognized Iris, yet he knew not by whom she had been sent. But he replied that he would quickly obey, whoever it was that thus called him to arms, and as he spoke, the goddess vanished into the heavens, forming in her ascent the beautiful rainbow, which was the sign of Juno's messenger.

> On equal wings she poised her weight,
> And formed a radiant rainbow in her flight.
> DRYDEN, *AEneid*, BOOK IX.

Then the warriors were called to action, and soon the whole army marched out into the open plain, Messapus, the Etrurian, commanding the front lines, the sons of Tyrrhus in the rear, and in the center Turnus himself. The Trojans within their camp, seeing the great cloud of dust which the tread of the hosts of the Latians raised on the plain, knew what it meant. Speedily they shut up their gates and set guards upon the walls, for AEneas at his departure had ordered them that in case of attack in his absence, they should not attempt a fight in the open field, but defend themselves within their ramparts. Turnus now tried to set fire to the Trojan fleet, which lay in the river close at hand, but the ships of AEneas could not be destroyed for they were made of wood cut from the forest of Cyb'e-le, the mother of the gods. When the hero was building them at the foot of Mount Ida, Cybele begged her son Jupiter, to grant that the vessels, being constructed of pine trees sacred to her, might be forever safe from destruction.

> "Grant me (she said) the sole request I bring,
> Since conquered heaven has owned you for its king.
> On Ida's brows, for ages past there stood,
> With firs and maples filled, a shady wood;
> And on the summit rose a sacred grove,

>   Where I was worshipped with religious love.
>   These woods, that holy grove, my long delight,
>   I gave the Trojan prince, to speed his flight.
>   Now filled with fear, on their behalf I come;
>   Let neither winds o'erset, nor waves entomb,
>   The floating forests of the sacred pine;
>   But let it be their safety to be mine."
>   DRYDEN, *AEneid*, BOOK XI.

This request, though coming from his mother, Jupiter was obliged to refuse, for it could not be, he said, that vessels built by mortal hands should be rendered immortal. He promised, however, that those of the Trojan ships which safely reached their destination in Italy should be transformed into goddesses or nymphs of the ocean. Therefore, when Turnus and his men rushed to the river with flaming torches, the time had come for the promise of the king of heaven to be fulfilled. As they were about to cast their firebrands upon the galleys a strange light flashed on the eyes of the Trojans, then a bright cloud shot across the sky, and from out of it these words uttered in a loud voice, were heard by the Trojans and Rutulians. "Men of Troy, you have no need to defend the ships. Sooner shall Turnus burn up the seas than those sacred pines. Glide on at your liberty, you nymphs of the main. It is the parent of the gods who commands you." No sooner were the words spoken than the ships all broke away from their fastenings, plunged out of sight into the depths of the river, and reappeared in a moment as beautiful maidens, moving gracefully along on the surface of the water.

>   No sooner had the goddess ceased to speak,
>   When, lo! the obedient ships their halsers break;
>   And strange to tell, like dolphins in the main
>   They plunge their prows, and dive and spring again;
>   As many beauteous maids the billows sweep,
>   As rode before tall vessels on the deep.
>   DRYDEN, *AEneid*, BOOK IX.

The Rutulians were astonished at this spectacle, but Turnus was still undismayed, and speaking to his people he declared that what they had just seen was bad for the Trojans themselves, for that now they had no longer means of escape, their ships having disappeared. "As for their much talked of destiny," said he, "it has been fulfilled, since they have reached the land of Italy. But I also have my destiny, and it is to destroy the accursed race. They depend a great deal on their walls, yet they have seen the walls of Troy go down in flames, though they were built by the hands of Neptune. I do not need arms made by Vulcan, nor shall we hide ourselves in a wooden horse. We shall fight the Trojans openly, and we shall teach them that they have not now to do with men like the Greeks, whom Hector baffled for ten years."

Turnus then laid siege to the Trojan camp. He placed sentinels outside the gates, and had watch-fires kindled at different points around the walls, after which his men lay down on the field to rest. But during the night the guards fell asleep, for they were fatigued after the labors of the day, and so the whole besieging army was now sunk in deep repose. The Trojans on the other hand kept strict watch within their camp, and adopted all necessary measures of defense.

> All things needful for defence abound;
> Mnestheus and brave Serestus walk the round,
> Commissioned by their absent prince to share
> The common danger, and divide the care.
> DRYDEN, *AEneid*, BOOK IX.1

The Trojan sentinels at one of the gates were Nisus and Euryalus— already mentioned as having taken part in the foot race at the funeral games.

> Love made them one in every thought;
> In battle side by side they fought;
> And now in duty at the gate
> The twain in common station wait.
> CONINGTON, *AEneid*, BOOK IX.

Now Nisus had conceived the idea of making his way through the Rutulian lines and conveying to AEneas at Pallanteum news of the dangerous situation of his people in the besieged camp, and he thought he would carry out his project while the enemy were all asleep outside the walls. Euryalus approved of the enterprise, and he begged that he himself might be permitted to take part in it. To this Nisus objected, for he did not wish that his dear young friend should be exposed to the danger of the undertaking. The mother of Euryalus had accompanied him all the way from Troy, and so great was her love for him that she refused to part from him even to share the good fortune of the other Trojan women who had settled in Sicily. Nisus was very unwilling to be the cause of grief to so devoted a mother, by permitting her son to join in an expedition in which he might lose his life.

> "Nor let me cause so dire a smart
> To that devoted mother's heart,
> Who, sole of all the matron train,
> Attends her darling o'er the main,
> Nor cares like others to sit down

An inmate of Acestes' town."
CONINGTON, *AEneid*, BOOK IX.

But Euryalus insisted on accompanying his friend, and so after obtaining the consent of the chiefs in command, who highly praised their courage and promised to reward them, they made ready to set forth. Euryalus begged that they would comfort and assist his mother if any evil should happen to him. To this request Iulus answered that she should be to him as if she were his own mother. "Gratitude is due to her," said he, "for having given birth to such a son. The reward I promise to give to you, if you return in safety, I shall give to your mother should ill fortune attend you."

Euryalus and Nisus now set out upon their mission. Passing through the camp of the sleeping Rutulians, they soon reached the outside of the enemy's lines. It happened that a body of Latian horsemen was just then passing that way on the route from Laurentum to join the army of Turnus. Catching sight of the two strangers, Volcens, the leader of the troop, cried out to them to "stand," and demanded to know who they were, and whither they were bound. The Trojans, making no answer, fled into a wood close by. Then Volcens placed guards on the passes and at the outlets of the wood to prevent the escape of the fugitives. Meanwhile Euryalus, getting separated from his companion, and losing his way in the thick shades of the forest, fell into the enemy's hands.

Nisus might have escaped, and had in fact got out of the wood, but finding that his friend had disappeared, he returned to search for him. Presently he heard the tramp of the horses, and looking forth from a thicket in which he had concealed himself, he saw Euryalus in the midst of the Latians, who were dragging him violently along. Deeply grieved at the sight, and resolving to rescue his comrade, or die in the attempt, Nisus, after praying to Diana, the goddess of the woods, to guide his weapon in its course, hurled a javelin at the enemy. It pierced the body of one of the Latians named Sulmo, who fell dead. His companions gazed around in amazement, not knowing whence the attack had come. Nisus then cast another javelin, and again one of the Latians fell to the ground. Enraged at seeing his men thus slain before his eyes by an unseen assailant, Volcens, with sword in hand, rushed upon Euryalus, crying out that his life should pay the penalty for both. Great was the agony of Nisus at seeing his friend about to be put to death, and starting from his concealment, he exclaimed aloud, "I am he who did the deed. Turn your arms therefore on me."

> "Me! me! (he cried) turn all your swords alone
> On me—the fact confessed, the fault my own.
> His only crime (if friendship can offend)

Is too much love to his unhappy friend."
DRYDEN, *AEneid*, BOOK IX.

But vain was the effort of Nisus to save his friend, for scarce had his last word been spoken when Euryalus fell lifeless to the earth, pierced by the weapon of Volcens. Filled with grief and rage, and eager to avenge the death of his companion, Nisus rushed into the midst of the foe, seeking only Volcens, and though blows showered upon him from all sides, he pressed on until coming up to the Latian chief, he slew him with a single thrust of his sword. Then covered with wounds, the brave Trojan dropped dead, falling upon the body of the friend he had so loved. Thus these two sons of Troy, companions in life, were companions also in death. Their friendship, immortalized by the Roman poet, became proverbial.

> O happy friends! for, if my verse can give
> Immortal life, your fame shall ever live,
> Fixed as the Capitol's foundation lies,
> And spread, where'er the Roman eagle flies!
> DRYDEN, *AEneid*, BOOK IX.

Early in the morning Turnus called his men to arms, and with loud shouts all rushed forward to the Trojan ramparts. Then a fierce conflict took place during which many heroes fell on both sides, after performing wonderful feats of valor. There was a wooden tower of great height and strength which stood outside the wall, and was connected with it by bridges. The Rutulians made great efforts to break down this tower, while the Trojans defended it by hurling stones upon the enemy, and casting darts at them through loopholes. So the struggle continued until Turnus with a flaming torch set the building on fire.

> Fierce Turnus first a firebrand flings;
> It strikes the sides, takes hold, and clings;
> The freshening breezes spread the blaze,
> And soon on plank and beam it preys.
> The inmates flutter in dismay
>   And vainly wish to fly;
> There as they huddle and retire
> Back to the part which 'scapes the fire,
> Sudden the o'erweighted mass gives way,
>   And falling, shakes the sky.
> CONINGTON, *AEneid*, BOOK IX.

Only two of the occupants of the tower—Hel'e-nor and Lycus—escaped destruction in its fall, but on emerging from the ruins they found themselves in the midst of the Rutulians. Helenor seeing no chance of saving his life, faced his foes like a lion and died in the thick of the fight.

Lycus, who was a swift runner, fled towards the walls, dashing through the lines of the enemy. He had almost grasped the summit of the rampart and reached the outstretched hands of his friends when Turnus, who had darted in pursuit, dragged him to the ground, and slew him, while he taunted him, saying, "Fool, didst thou hope to be able to escape our hands?"

The battle now became more furious. From every quarter were heard shouts of fighting men and clashing of arms. Amongst the heroes of the day was young Iulus, hitherto accustomed to use his weapons only in the chase. His first arrow in war was now aimed against the brother-in-law of Turnus, a chief named Nu-ma'nus, who fought not only with sword but with his tongue, mocking at the Trojans in a loud voice, in front of the Latian lines. "Are you not ashamed, Trojans," cried he, "to be a second time shut up behind walls? What madness has brought you to Italy? Know that it is not Grecians, nor the crafty Ulysses, you have now to deal with. We are a hardy race. We dip our infants in the rivers to inure them to cold. Our boys are trained to hunt in the woods. Our whole life is spent in arms. Age does not impair our courage or vigor. As for you, your very dress is embroidered with yellow and purple; indolence is your delight; you love to indulge in dancing and such frivolous pleasures. Women you are, and not men. Leave fighting to warriors and handle not the sword."

> "Leave men, like us, in arms to deal
> Nor bruise your lily hands with steel."
> CONINGTON, *AEneid*, BOOK IX.

The spirited young Trojan prince could not patiently endure these insults, and so drawing his bow-string and praying to Father Jupiter, he sent forth his steel-tipped arrow. Whizzing through the air the weapon pierced the head of Numanus, and at the same moment Iulus exclaimed, "Vain boaster, this is our answer to your insults." With shouts of joy the Trojans applauded the deed, and loud were their praises of the valor of their young chief. Even from on high came approving words, for just then the fair-haired Apollo, seated on a cloud, was watching the conflict. And thus spoke the god in a loud voice, "Go on and increase in valor, O youth. Such is the path-way to immortality, thou art the descendant of gods, and from whom gods are to descend."

[Illustration with caption: APOLLO VANISHING AFTER CAUTIONING IULUS.
(Drawn by Trautschold)]

Uttering these words Apollo came down from the sky, and taking the appearance of Bu'tes, formerly the armor-bearer of Anchises, but now the guardian of Iulus, walked by the young prince's side and addressed him, saying, "Son of AEneas, let it be enough for thee that by thine arrow

Numanus has fallen. Apollo has granted to thee this glory; but take no further part in the conflict." Then the god, throwing off his disguise, ascended to the heavens. The Trojan chiefs recognized him as he departed, and thus knowing that it was the divine will, they caused Iulus to retire, while they themselves again rushed forward to the battle—

> They bend their bows; they whirl their slings around;
> Heaps of spent arrows fall, and strew the ground;
> And helms, and shields, and rattling arms, resound.
> DRYDEN, *AEneid*, BOOK IX.

At this point two brothers, Pan'da-rus and Bit'i-as, sons of the Trojan Al-ca'non, of Mount Ida, tall and powerful youths, threw open the gate at which they were posted as sentinels, and standing within, one on each side, they challenged the foe to enter. The Rutulians rushed forward as soon as they saw the passage open. Several of them were slain at the threshold by the valiant brothers. Then some of the Trojans sallied out beyond the rampart, and a fierce fight took place. King Turnus, hearing of these events, hurried to the gate, and joining in the battle, slew many of the Trojan warriors. He hurled a dart at Bitias, and so great was the force of the blow that not even the huge sentinel's shield, formed of two bull's hides, nor his breastplates with double scales of gold, could resist it.

> Not two bull-hides the impetuous force withhold,
> Nor coat of double mail, with scales of gold.
> Down sunk the monster-bulk, and pressed the ground,
> His arms and clattering shield on the vast body sound
> DRYDEN, *AEneid*, BOOK IX.

When Pandarus beheld his brother stretched dead on the ground, and saw that the battle was going against the Trojans, he closed the gate, moving it upon its hinges and fastening it in its place with the strength of his broad shoulders. Some of his own people were thus shut out and left in the midst of the enemy, but in his hurry Pandarus did not notice that amongst those who were shut in was the fierce King Turnus.

> Fond fool! amidst the noise and din
> He saw not Turnus rushing in,
> But closed him in the embattled hold,
> A tiger in a helpless fold.
> CONINGTON, *AEneid*, BOOK IX.

As soon as Pandarus saw what had happened, he hurled a spear with mighty force at the Rutulian king, eager to avenge his brother's death, but Juno turning the weapon aside, it struck into the gate, where it remained fixed. Then Turnus slew Pandarus with a swift stroke of his sword, exclaiming, "Not so shall you escape." The Trojans who witnessed the deed, fled terrified from the spot, and if Turnus at this moment had opened the gate and admitted his Rutulian warriors, that day would have been the last of the war and of the Trojan race.

> The Trojans fly in wild dismay,
>   O, then had Turnus thought
> To force the fastenings of the gates
> And call within his valiant mates,
> The nation and the war that day
>   Alike to end had brought!
>   CONINGTON, *AEneid*, BOOK IX.

But Turnus thought only of slaying his foes who were at hand and so he speedily put many of them to the sword. The Trojan chiefs Mnestheus and Sergestus, as soon as they heard that their people were fleeing before the Rutulian king, hastened up and reproved them in severe words. "Whither do you flee?" cried Mnestheus. "What other fortifications have you but this? Shall one man be permitted to work such destruction in our camp? Are you not ashamed? Have you no regard for your unhappy country, your ancient gods, or your great leaders?"

Touched by these words, and inspired with fresh courage, the Trojans formed themselves into a solid body. Then turning round they made a firm stand against the Rutulian chief, who now began to retreat towards that part of the camp which was bounded by the river. The Trojans advanced upon him with loud shouts, yet the brave king would fain have resisted. As when a troop of hunters press upon a fierce lion, the savage animal, too courageous to fly, yet dares not face the numbers and weapons of his assailants, so Turnus with reluctant steps drew backwards; yet twice again he attacked the Trojans and twice drove them along the walls. At length gathering from all parts of the camp, the Trojans made a united advance and Turnus, no longer able to withstand the assaults of his foes, fled to the river, and plunging in, was soon in the midst of his friends who received him with joyous acclamation.

O'er all his limbs dark sweat-drops break;
No time to breathe; thick pantings shake
    His vast and laboring frame.
At length, accoutred as he stood,
Headlong he plunged into the flood.
The yellow flood the charge received,
With buoyant tide his weight upheaved,
And cleansing off the encrusted gore,
Returned him to his friends once more.
    CONINGTON, *AEneid*, BOOK IX.

IX. THE COUNCIL OF THE GODS—RETURN OF AENEAS—BATTLE ON THE SHORE—DEATH OF PALLAS.

Meanwhile the king of heaven who had been watching the conflict on the banks of the Tiber, called a council of the gods to consider whether it would not be well to put an end to the quarrel between Juno and Venus over the fortunes of the Trojans. The divinities assembled in their golden council chamber on Mount Olympus and Jupiter addressed them. "Ye gods," said he, "why do you seek to alter the decrees of heaven? It was my desire that the Italians should not make war upon the men of Troy. Why then have you incited them to arms? The time for conflict between the two races favored by Juno and Venus has not yet come. That time will be hereafter when the Carthaginians shall put forth their efforts to ruin Rome. Then indeed you shall be free to take either side in the contest. For the present cease your quarrels, and let the league agreed upon between AEneas and Latinus be ratified."

Thus spoke the king of heaven. Then Venus addressed the gods in behalf of her son, whose sufferings, she said, were due to the hatred of Juno. She recounted the various attempts of the unforgiving queen to destroy the Trojans—how AEolus at her bidding had sent his storms to scatter the fleet of AEneas, how Iris, her messenger, had induced the Trojan women to set fire to the ships at Drepanum, and how at her request the Fury Alecto had incited Queen Amata and King Turnus to war against the men of Troy.

Juno next addressed the council, and spoke many bitter words against AEneas and the Trojans, who, she declared, were themselves to blame for all the evils that had come upon them. The Greek war against Troy had not been caused by her, but by the Trojan Paris, and for his conduct in carrying off Helen, Venus was responsible. As to the troubles in Italy, it was true that AEneas had sailed to that country by the will of the fates, but why, she asked, did he stir up war among Italian nations that had before been at peace.

Juno having finished her speech against the Trojans, and none of the other divinities desiring to take part in the controversy, Jupiter then delivered judgment, declaring that as the quarrel between the two goddesses could not be amicably settled, nor peace brought about between the Trojans and Italians, the fates should take their course.

> "Since Troy with Latium must contend,
> And these your wranglings find no end,
> Let each man use his chance to day
> And carve his fortune as he may;
> Each warrior from his own good lance
> Shall reap the fruit of toil or chance;
> Jove deals to all an equal lot,
> And Fate shall loose or cut the knot."
>   CONINGTON, *AEneid*, BOOK IX.

Thus ended the council of the gods, and so by the decree of the king of heaven the quarrel between the Trojans and Italians was left to the fortune of war.

Meanwhile the Trojans in the camp on the Tiber were being hard pressed by the enemy. As soon as Turnus had rejoined his army, the attack on the ramparts was renewed with increased vigor, and the brave Mnestheus and his companions, their forces now much reduced in number, were beginning to lose hope.

> Hopeless of flight, more hopeless of relief,
> Thin on the towers they stand; and e'en those few,
> A feeble, fainting, and dejected crew.
>   DRYDEN, AEneid, BOOK X.

But AEneas was hastening to the rescue. Having formed the league with Tarchon, he lost no time in preparing to return to his friends. Many other chiefs of Etruria joined their forces to the expedition, and all placed themselves under the command of AEneas, in accordance with the will of the gods that only under a foreign leader could they be successful in the war against the Rutulians.

When everything was ready for departure they embarked on a fleet of thirty ships, and sailed down the Tyr-rhe'ni-an Sea, along the Etrurian coast, towards the mouth of the Tiber. AEneas led the way in his own galley, and with him was young Pallas, the son of Evander. During the voyage he learned in a strange manner of the perilous situation of his people in the camp. It was night, and as he was seated at the helm, for his anxiety permitted him not to sleep, a number of sea-nymphs appeared swimming by the side of his ship. One of them, Cym-o-do-ce'a by name, grasped the stern of the vessel with her right hand, while with her left she gently rowed her way through the waves. Then she addressed the Trojan chief. "Son of the gods," said she, "we are the pines of Mount Ida, at one time your fleet, but now nymphs of the sea. The Rutulian king would have destroyed us with fire had it not been permitted to us by the mother of the gods to burst our cables, and assume our present form. We come to tell you that your son

Ascanius is besieged in the camp, and pressed on all sides by the Latian foe. Be ready then at the dawn of morning with your troops, and bear with you to the fight the arms and armor which Vulcan has made. To-morrow's sun shall see many of the Rutulian enemy slain."

> She ceased, and parting, to the bark
>   A measured impulse gave;
> Like wind-swift arrow to its mark
>   It darts along the wave.
> The rest pursue. In wondering awe
> The chief revolves the things he saw.
>   CONINGTON, *AEneid*, BOOK X.

At dawn of morning the fleet came within view of the Trojan camp. Then AEneas standing on the deck of his own vessel, held aloft his bright shield made by Vulcan. His people saw it from the ramparts, and shouted loud with joy, and now, their hope being revived, they assailed the enemy with fresh courage. The Rutulians and Latians were amazed at this sudden change, not knowing the cause, but looking back, they too beheld the fleet approaching the shore.

The brave Turnus however was not dismayed at the sight. On the contrary he resolved to give battle to the new foe without delay, and so addressing his men he bade them fight valiantly for their homes and country, remembering the glorious deeds of their ancestors.

> "Your sires, your sons, your houses, and your lands,
> And dearest wives, are all within your hands;
> Be mindful of the race from whence you came,
> And emulate in armsl your fathers' fame."
>   DRYDEN, *AEneid*, BOOK X.

Then he hurried to the shore with the main body of his army, and AEneas having already landed his companions and allies, a fierce battle began. The Trojan hero performed wonderful feats of valor. First he attacked the Latian troops, who were in front of the hosts of the enemy, and he slew their leader The'ron, a warrior of giant size. Through his brazen shield and golden coat of mail AEneas smote him with his sword. Next he slew Lycas, and then Cis'seus and Gyas, tall men and powerful, who, with clubs like the club of Hercules, had been striking down the Trojans. Then a band of seven warrior brothers, the sons of Phorcus, attacked the Trojan chief, hurling seven darts upon him all together, some of which rebounded from his shield, and some, turned aside by Venus, harmlessly grazed his skin. AEneas now called to the faithful Achates to bring him darts—those with which on the plains of Troy the bodies of Grecian warriors had been pierced—

> "Those fatal weapons, which, inured to blood,
> In Grecian bodies under Ilium stood;
> Not one of those my hand shall toss in vain
> Against our foes, on this contended plain."
>   DRYDEN, *AEneid*, BOOK X.

Grasping a mighty spear, as soon as these weapons were brought to him, AEneas hurled it at Macon, one of the brothers. It pierced through his shield and breastplate, and he fell mortally wounded. At his brother Alcanor, who had run to his relief, AEneas cast another dart, which penetrated his shoulder, leaving the warrior's arm hanging lifeless by his body. And now Hal-ae'sus with his Auruncian bands, and Messapus, the son of Neptune, conspicuous with his steeds, hastened up to encounter AEneas. The fight then became more furious and many were slain on both sides.

> Thus Trojan and Italian meet,
> With face to face, and feet to feet,
>   And hand close pressed to hand.
>   CONINGTON, *AEneid*, BOOK X.

In another quarter of the field young Pallas, fighting at the head of his Arcadian horsemen, slew many chiefs of the Latians and Rutulians. Opposed to him was Lausus, son of the tyrant Mezentius. Lausus being hard pressed by the Arcadians, King Turnus was called to his assistance, and rushing up he cried to the Rutulians, "Desist you for a moment from the battle. I alone will fight Pallas. Would that his father were here to see." Hearing these words the brave son of Evander advanced boldly into the open plain between the two hosts. The hearts of his Arcadian followers were filled with dread at seeing their young chief about to engage in single combat with so great a warrior as the Rutulian king. Turnus sprang down from his chariot, to meet his foe on foot.

> And, as a lion—when he spies from far
> A bull that seems to meditate the war,
> Bending his neck, and spurning back the sand—
> Runs roaring downward from his hilly stand;
> Imagine eager Turnus not more slow
> To rush from high on his unequal foe.
>   DRYDEN, *AEneid*, BOOK X.

Then Pallas prayed to Hercules, once his father's guest, to help him. Hercules in his place in heaven, hearing the prayer, groaned in distress and poured forth tears, for he knew that the fate of the brave youth could not be averted. Noticing the grief of his son, almighty Father Jupiter spoke to him in comforting words. "To every one," said he, "his period of life is fixed. Short is the time allotted to all, but it is the part of the brave man to lengthen out fame by glorious deeds. Many even of the sons of the gods have fallen under the lofty walls of Troy. Turnus too awaits his destiny, and already he has nearly arrived at the limit of existence left to him." So saying the king of heaven turned his eyes from the scene of battle.

Pallas now hurled his spear with great force. The weapon struck the armor of Turnus near his shoulder, and piercing through it, grazed his body. Then Turnus poising his sharp steel-tipped javelin, darted it at Pallas. Through the centre of his many-plated shield and the folds of his corselet the fatal shaft passed into the breast of the brave youth, inflicting a mortal wound. Down on the earth he fell, and Turnus approaching the dead body exclaimed, "You Arcadians carry these my words to your king. In such plight as he deserved I send his son back to him. His league of friendship with AEneas shall cost him dear."

[Illustration with caption: PALLAS' BODY BORNE FROM THE FIELD. (Drawn by Birch.)]

Then Turnus stripped from the body of Pallas a beautiful belt, embossed with figures carved in gold, and putting it on his own armor, triumphed in the spoil. It proved to be a fatal possession for Turnus.

> O mortals! blind in fate who never know
> To bear high fortune, or endure the low!
> The time shall come when Turnus, but in vain,
> Shall wish untouched the trophies of the slain—
> Shall wish the fatal belt were far away,
> And curse the dire remembrance of the day.
> DRYDEN, *AEneid*, BOOK X.

The body of the brave young prince was laid upon his shield, and borne away from the field of battle, accompanied by a numerous retinue of his sorrowing friends.

> O sad, proud thought, that thus a son
>   Should reach a father's door!
> This day beheld your wars begun;
>   This day beholds them o'er,
> CONINGTON, *AEneid*, BOOK X.

The news of the fate of Pallas soon reached AEneas, who was deeply distressed at the thought of the sorrow the youth's death would bring upon his aged father Evander. Eager for vengeance, he hastened through the battle field in search of Turnus, slaying many chiefs of the enemy whom he encountered on his way. But he was not yet to meet the Rutulian king face to face, for Juno, by Jupiter's permission, led Turnus off the field, and saved him for a time from the wrath of the Trojan hero. Out of a hollow cloud she fashioned a phantom with the shape, likeness and voice of AEneas, and caused it to appear before Turnus, as if challenging him to combat.

> A phantom in AEneas' mould
> She fashions, wondrous to behold,
>   Of hollow shadowy cloud,
> Bids it the Dardan arms assume,
> The shield, the helmet, and the plume,
> Gives soulless words of swelling tone,
> And motions like the hero's own,
>   As stately and as proud.
>   CONINGTON, *AEneid*, BOOK X.

The Rutulian king bravely advanced to attack the supposed Trojan chief, upon which the spectre, wheeling about, hastily retreated towards the river. Turnus followed, loudly upbraiding AEneas as a coward. It happened that at the shore there was a ship, connected with the land by a plank bridge or gangway. Into this ship the phantom fled, closely pursued by Turnus; and no sooner had the latter reached the deck of the vessel than Juno, bursting the cables which held it to the bank, sent it floating down the stream. Then the figure of cloud, soaring aloft, vanished into the air, and Turnus knew that he had been deceived.

He was much distressed at being thus separated from his brave followers, and mortified at the thought that they might think he had deserted them in the hour of danger. In his grief he attempted to destroy his own life with his sword, but Juno restrained him, and the ship, wafted along by favoring wind and tide, bore him to Ardea, the capital city of his own country, where his father, King Daunus, resided.

Meanwhile, on the battle field, the Etrurian king, Mezentius, who had taken the place of Turnus, attacked the Trojans with great fury. He had slain many valiant warriors when AEneas espying him from a distance, hurried forward to encounter him. Mezentius stood firm, and relying on his strong arm and his weapons, rather than on divine aid (being a despiser of the gods) he cast a spear at the Trojan leader. The missile struck the hero's shield, but it was the shield which Vulcan had made, and could not be pierced by earthly weapon. Then AEneas hurled his javelin. Through the triple plates of brass, and the triple bull-hide covering of the Etrurian king's shield it passed, and, lodging in his groin, inflicted a severe, though not fatal, wound. Instantly the Trojan chief rushed, with sword in hand, upon his foe, as, disabled, he was about to withdraw from the conflict. But at this moment young Lausus, the son of Mezentius, sprang forward and received on his sword the blow that had been intended for his father.

> The pious youth, resolved on death, below
> The lifted sword, springs forth to face the foe;
> Protects his parent, and prevents the blow.
>   DRYDEN, *AEneid*, BOOK X.

But Lausus was no match for the veteran Trojan warrior. Yet AEneas, admiring his courage and filial devotion, would fain have spared the brave youth. "Why do you attempt," said he, "what you have not strength to accomplish? You do but rush to your own destruction." Regardless, however, of danger, the gallant Lausus fought till he fell lifeless on the earth. AEneas was touched with pity at the sight, for he thought of his own son, and of how he himself had loved his own father. Then, he tenderly lifted the body from the ground, and consigned it to the care of his friends. They carried it to Mezentius, who was resting on the river bank, after having bathed his wounds in the water. When he beheld the lifeless form, the unhappy man burst into tears, and bitterly lamented his own misdeeds which had brought such calamities upon him—banishment from his throne and country, and now, worst of all, the loss of his son. "Why do I live, my son," cried he, "at the cost of thy life? My crimes have been the cause of thy death."

> "Dear child! I stained your glorious name
> By my own crimes, driven out to shame
> From my ancestral reign;
> My country's vengeance claimed my blood;
> Ah! had that tainted, guilty flood
>   Been shed from every vein!
> Now 'mid my kind I linger still
> And live; but leave the light I will."
>   CONINGTON, *AEneid*, BOOK X.

Then though he was suffering much from the pain of his wound, he called for his horse, the gallant steed Rhoebus, which had borne him victorious through many a fight. The animal seemed to feel the grief of its master, and to understand the words he spoke: "Long, Rhoebus," said he, "have we lived, companions in war,—if indeed the life of mortals can be said to be long. But to-day we shall either die together, or bear away the body of AEneas, and so avenge the death of Lausus."

Mounting his horse, and filling both hands with javelins Mezentius then rode rapidly to the scene of conflict, calling loudly for AEneas. The Trojan chief knew the voice, and eager for the encounter, he quickly advanced. But the brave Etrurian, fearing not to meet his foe, cried out, "Cruel man, you cannot terrify me, now that my son is snatched from me. I am not afraid of death, for I have come to die. First, however, take these gifts which I bring for you." Thus speaking he hurled a dart at the Trojan leader, and then another and another, and three times he rode in a circle round the hero, casting javelins at him. But the weapons of Mezentius could not pass through the celestial shield of AEneas, though they fixed themselves in it, and there were so many that they resembled a grove of spears.

> Thrice, fiercely hurling spears on spears,
>   From right to left he wheeled;
> Thrice, facing round as he careers,
> The steely grove the Trojan bears,
>   Thick planted on his shield.

At length AEneas hurled a javelin at the warrior's horse, striking it between the temples. The animal reared, beating the air with its hoofs, and rolling over its rider, pinned him to the earth. Then the Trojan chief rushed, sword in hand, upon his fallen foe, and the brave Mezentius died asking only the favor of burial for his body.

> "For this, this only favor, let me sue;
> If pity can to conquered foes be due,
> Refuse it not; but let my body have
> The last retreat of human-kind, a grave.
> This refuge for my poor remains provide;
> And lay my much-loved Lausus by my side."
>   DRYDEN, *AEneid*, BOOK X.

X. FUNERAL OF PALLAS—AENEAS AND TURNUS FIGHT—TURNUS IS SLAIN.

With the death of Mezentius the battle of the day came to an end. Early next morning AEneas offered sacrifices to the gods in thanksgiving for his victory. On a rising ground he caused to be erected the trunk of a huge oak, with its boughs lopped off. Upon this he hung as an offering to the war-god Mars, the arms that had been borne by the Etrurian king—his crest, and his broken spears, his breastplate, showing the marks of many blows, his shield of brass, and his ivory-hilted sword. Then he spoke words of encouragement to his chiefs and companions.

"Brother warriors, our most important work is done. Henceforth we need have no fear. Having vanquished the tyrant Mezentius, the way lies open for us to the Latian capital. Make ready your arms so that there may be no obstacle to detain us when the proper moment arrives for leading forth our valiant youth from the camp. Meanwhile let us commit to the earth the bodies of our dead friends. It is the sole honor remaining for us to pay to the heroic men who, with their lives, have won for us a country to dwell in.

But first, to the mourning city of Evander let the body of the noble Pallas be conveyed."

> "Brave Pallas, heir of high renown,
> Whose hopeful day has set too soon,
> O'ercast by darkness ere its noon"
> CONINGTON, *AEneid*, BOOK X.

The obsequies of the young prince were carried out on a scale of great magnificence. A thousand men formed the funeral procession. The body was dressed in rich robes, stiff with embroidery of gold and purple, which Queen Dido with her own hands had wrought for AEneas. Beside the bier were borne the dead youth's arms, and the spoils he had won in battle. His war-horse AEthon, too, was led along, big tear drops running down the animal's cheeks, as if it shared in the general sorrow.

> Then AEthon comes, his trappings doffed,
> The warrior's gallant horse;
> Big drops of pity oft and oft
> Adown his visage course.
> CONINGTON, *AEneid*, BOOK XI.

Behind followed the numerous escort of Trojan, Etrurian and Arcadian warriors, and the long procession passed on with a last sad adieu from the Trojan chief. "By the same fearful fate of war," said he, "I am called to other scenes of woe. Farewell, noble Pallas, farewell, forever." When the sorrowing cortege reached Pallanteum, the whole city was in mourning. To the gates the people hastened in vast numbers bearing funeral torches in their hands, according to ancient custom, and Trojans and Arcadians joined in loud lamentations.

> Both parties meet; they raise a doleful cry;
> The matrons from the walls with shrieks reply;
> And their mixed mourning rends the vaulted sky.
> DRYDEN, *AEneid*, BOOK XI.

King Evander distracted with grief, prostrated himself upon the bier, and clasping in his arms the body of his son, poured out a flood of tears, bewailing the unhappy fate which left him childless in his old age.

Meantime, AEneas and the Latian chiefs agreed upon a truce of twelve days for the burial of the dead of both armies, which lay scattered over the battle field. While this sad duty was being performed, King Latinus and his counsellors considered what was best to be done, after the truce—whether to continue the war, or to propose terms of peace. They had sent ambassadors to solicit help from Di-o-me'de, one of the Grecian heroes of the Trojan war, who, after the siege, had settled in Apulia in Italy, and built the city of Ar-gyr'i-pa, where he now resided. But Diomede refused to fight against AEneas, and he reminded the Latians that all who had raised the sword against Troy had suffered grievous punishments. "I myself," said he, "am an exile from my native country, and dire calamities have fallen upon many of my people. Ask me not, therefore, to quarrel with the Trojans. How mighty their leader is in battle I know by experience, for I have engaged him hand to hand. Had Troy produced two other such heroes, it would have fared ill with Greece. It was Hector and AEneas who held back the victory of our countrymen for ten years—both distinguished for valor and noble feats of arms, but the son of Anchises excelling in reverence for the gods. With him, therefore, men of Latium, I advise you to join in a league of friendship, if by any means you can do it. Beware, however, of encountering him in war."

The ambassadors delivered this message to King Latinus as he was sitting in his council chamber with his chief men around him. The king once more earnestly advised that they should make peace with the Trojans, and give them lands to settle on, if they still desired to dwell in Latium, or build for them a new fleet if they were willing to withdraw from Italy and seek homes in some other country. He also advised that they should send these proposals to the Trojan camp.

> "To treat the peace, a hundred senators
> Shall be commissioned hence with ample powers,
> With olive crowned; the presents they shall bear,
> A purple robe, a royal ivory chair,
> And sums of gold. Among yourselves debate
> This great affair, and save the sinking state."
> DRYDEN, *AEneid*, BOOK XI.

King Turnus was present at this council, and there was also present a Latian named Dran'ces, a very eloquent man, but not a warrior.

> —Bold at the council board,
> But cautious in the field, he shunned the sword.
> DRYDEN, *AEneid*, BOOK XI.

Drances spoke in support of the advice given by Latinus. He also said that one more gift should be sent to AEneas, namely, the fair Lavinia, since by no other means could peace be more firmly established than by a marriage between the Latian princess and the Trojan hero. Then addressing Turnus, the bold Drances reproached him with having brought upon his country all the horrors of war to gratify his ambition for the honor of a royal wife. "You Turnus," said he, "are the cause of the evils which afflict us. It is through you that so many of our chiefs have perished on the battle field, and that our whole city is in mourning. Have you no pity for your own people? Lay aside your fierceness, and give up this hopeless contest. But if you are still eager for glory in war, and must have a kingdom with your wife, then take all the risk yourself, and do not ask others to expose themselves to danger for you. AEneas has challenged you to single combat. If you have any valor, go and fight with him."

Enraged at this speech, Turnus angrily replied—"Drances, you have always many words when deeds are required. But this is not the time to fill the chamber with words, which come in torrents from you so long as you are in safety with strong walls between you and the foe. You charge me with cowardice, you, the valiant Drances, whose right hand, forsooth, has piled up so many trophies of victory on the field! There is an opportunity for you now, however, to put your valor to the proof, for we have not far to go in search of the enemy. Why do you hesitate to march against them?"

Then speaking to the king, Turnus earnestly entreated him not to give up the fight because of one defeat. "We have still," said he, "ample resources and fresh troops, and many Italian cities and nations are in alliance with us. The Trojans as well as ourselves have suffered heavy loss. Why then should we permit fear to overcome us almost at the beginning of the struggle? If the Trojans demand that I alone shall fight their leader, gladly will I advance against him, even though he prove himself as great a warrior as Achilles, and sheath himself in armor forged by the hands of Vulcan."

Turnus had scarcely finished speaking, when a messenger rushed into the palace with the alarming intelligence that the Trojan and Etrurian armies had quitted their camp on the bank of the Tiber, and were marching toward the city. Instantly all was confusion and dismay in the council.

> A turmoil takes the public mind;
> Their passions flame, by furious wind
>   To conflagration blown;
> At once to arms they fain would fly;
> "To arms!" the youth impatient cry;
>   The old men weep and moan.
>   CONINGTON, *AEneid*, BOOK XI.

Turnus was quick to take advantage of this altered state of affairs. "Citizens," he exclaimed, "will you still persist in talking about peace even now that the enemy is almost at your doors?" Then, withdrawing from the council chamber, he hastened to give orders to his Rutulian chiefs to get the troops ready for immediate action—some to lead the armed horsemen out upon the plain, others to man the towers, others to follow him where he should command. The Latians, too, excited to ardor by the approach of the enemy, rushed to arms, and soon the whole city was in warlike commotion.

> Some help to sink new trenches; others aid
> To ram the stones, or raise the palisade.
> Hoarse trumpets sound the alarm; around the walls
> Runs a distracted crew, whom their last labor calls.
>   DRYDEN, *AEneid*, BOOK XI.

In the midst of the excitement, Queen Amata and her daughter Lavinia, attended by a great number of matrons, repaired in procession to the temple of Minerva, and prayed to the goddess, to break the Trojan pirate's spear, and lay him prostrate in death under the city's walls. Meanwhile, Turnus, armed for battle, went forth from the palace, and hastened towards the plain to join his brave Rutulians. At the gate he was met by the Volscian Queen Camilla, at the head of a troop of female warriors, all on horseback. The brave queen requested that she and her companions should have the honor of being the first to encounter the Trojan host. "Noble heroine," replied the Rutulian chief, "how can I express my thanks? Since such is your spirit, I am willing that you should share the dangers with us. AEneas has sent his horsemen to scour the plain, while he himself is marching through a secluded valley with his foot soldiers to take the city by surprise. This we learn from our scouts. Now I will beset him on the way with an armed band, and to you I assign the task of engaging the Etrurian horsemen. The brave Messapus and the Latian troops will be with you, and under your command."

Camilla and her troop performed prodigies of valor in the battle which now took place on the plain before the city. Many Trojan and Etrurian warriors fell, stricken down by the darts or pierced by the sword of the brave heroine. On both sides the battle was maintained with the utmost bravery. Twice the Trojans and their Tuscan allies drove the Latians flying to the walls, and twice the Latians, facing about, furiously drove back the Trojans.

> Twice were the Tuscans masters of the field,
> Twice by the Latins, in their turn, repelled.
> Ashamed at length, to the third charge they ran—
> Both hosts resolved, and mingled man to man.
> Now dying groans are heard; the fields are strewed,
> With falling bodies, and are drunk with blood.
> Arms, horses, men, on heaps together lie;
> Confused the fight, and more confused the cry.
>   DRYDEN, *AEneid*, BOOK XI.

The battle continued to rage furiously, and it seemed doubtful which side would win, until Camilla was slain by the Etruscan Aruns, who had been watching for an opportunity to cast a spear at the queen.

> This way and that his winding course he bends,
> And wheresoe'er she turns, her steps attends.
>   DRYDEN, *AEneid*, BOOK XI.

There was in the Trojan army a warrior, and priest of Cybele, named Chlo'reus, conspicuous on the field by the rich trappings of his horse and his own glittering arms and attire. He wore a purple robe, his helmet and the bow which hung from his shoulders were of gold; his saffron colored scarf was fastened with a gold clasp; and his tunic was embroidered with needle-work. Camilla seeing these beautiful and costly things, became eager to possess them, and so she pursued Chloreus over the field of battle.

> Him the fierce maid beheld with ardent eyes,
> Fond and ambitious of so rich a prize,
> Blind in her haste, she chases him alone,
> And seeks his life, regardless of her own.
>   DRYDEN, *AEneid*, BOOK XI.

Thus she furnished the opportunity desired by Aruns, who, from a covert in which he lay concealed, hurled a dart at the queen as, heedless of danger, she rode in pursuit of Chloreus. The weapon pierced her body and she sank down lifeless.

The fortune of the day now turned to the side of the Trojans. Dismayed by the loss of their brave leader Camilla, the Volscian troops fled from the field. The Rutulian captains, also losing courage, sought safety in flight, and soon the whole Italian army was in full retreat towards the city, hotly pursued by the Trojans. At the gates many were trampled to death in the wild rush to get within, while many more were slain by the swords of the enemy pressing on behind.

> Then, in a fright, the folding gates they close,
> But leave their friends excluded with their foes.
> The vanquished cry; the victors loudly shout;
> 'Tis terror all within, and slaughter all without.
>   DRYDEN, *AEneid*, BOOK XI.

When Turnus heard that Camilla had fallen, that the Trojans had been victorious in the battle, and that all was confusion and terror within the walls, he immediately quitted the post where he had been lying in wait for AEneas, and hurried towards the city. Almost at the same moment the Trojan chief issued forth from the valley. Both armies and both leaders were now in sight of each other and both were eager for battle, but night coming on, they pitched their tents and encamped in front of the town.

But the Latians were now disheartened, and Turnus saw they were no longer willing to continue a struggle which seemed hopeless. He himself, however, was still determined not to yield, and he resolved to encounter AEneas in single combat. "With my own right hand," said he, "I shall slay the Trojan adventurer, while the Latians sit still and look on, and if he vanquish me, let him rule over us, and have Lavinia for his bride." King Latinus endeavored to dissuade him from this dangerous enterprise. "Turnus," said he, "you are heir to the kingdom of your father Daunus. There are other high-born maidens in Latium, from whom you may chose a wife. It was decreed by the gods that Lavinia should wed no prince of Italy, yet through affection for you, and yielding to the prayers of my queen, I permitted the Latians to make war against him to whom, in accordance with the will of heaven, my daughter was promised. You see what calamities have come upon us in consequence. In two great battles we have been defeated, and now we are scarce able to defend ourselves in our capital city. If upon your death I am resolved to make an alliance with the Trojans, is it not better to put an end to the war while you are still alive?"

Queen Amata also entreated Turnus not to risk his life in an engagement with the Trojan chief. "Whatever fortune awaits you, Turnus," she said, "awaits me also. I shall not live and see AEneas my son-in-law." The fair Lavinia was present during her mother's passionate appeal, but she expressed her feeling only by tears and modest blushes.

>   —A flood of tears Lavinia shed;
> A crimson blush her beauteous face o'erspread,
> Varying her cheeks by turns with white and red.
> Delightful change! Thus Indian ivory shows,
> Which with the bordering paint of purple glows;
> Or lilies damasked by the neighboring rose.
>   DRYDEN, *AEneid*, BOOK XII.

But Turnus would not listen to the advice of King Latinus or Queen Amata and so he sent his herald Idmon with a challenge to AEneas. "Tell him," said he, "not to lead his men against the Rutulians to-morrow. Let both our armies rest, while by his sword and mine the war shall be decided." AEneas, who had himself already proposed this method of settling the quarrel, rejoiced to hear that now at length the war was to be brought to an end on such terms. He therefore gladly accepted the challenge, and early next morning preparations were made for the combat.

A space of ground was measured off on the open plain in front of the city walls, and in the center were erected altars of turf. The two armies were marshalled on opposite sides of this space, the Trojans and Etrurians on one side, the Rutulians and Latians on the other, and at a given signal every man fixed his spear in the earth, and laid down his shield. On the towers and house tops the women and old men crowded to witness the fight. King

Latinus rode out from the city in a chariot drawn by four horses, and wearing on his head a crown with twelve rays of gold. Turnus rode in a chariot drawn by two white steeds, and he bore in each hand a javelin tipped with steel. On the other side, AEneas, brilliant in the arms which Vulcan had made, advanced from his camp into the open space, accompanied by the young Iulus. Then the customary sacrifices and offerings were made at the altars, after which the Trojan chief, unsheathing his sword, prayed aloud to the gods, and pledged his people to the conditions of the combat:—

"If victory in this fight shall fall to Turnus, the Trojans shall retire to Evander's city, and no more make war on the Latians or Rutulians. But if victory fall to our side, even then I shall not compel the Italians to be subject to the Trojans, for I desire not empire for myself. Both nations shall enter into alliance on equal terms, and Latinus shall still be king. The Trojans shall build a city for me, and to it Lavinia shall give her name."

Then Latinus calling on the gods to hear his words, and laying his hand upon the altar, swore for himself and his people that they would never violate the treaty of peace, no matter how the combat of the day should result.

> "By the same heaven (said he), and earth, and main,
> And all the powers that all the three contain;
> Whatever chance befall on either side,
> No term of time this union shall divide;
> No force, no fortune, shall my vows unbind,
> Or shake the steadfast tenor of my mind."
> DRYDEN, *AEneid*, BOOK XII.

But while the solemn ceremonies were being carried out at the altars, the Rutulians began to show signs of dissatisfaction. It seemed to them that the youthful Turnus was no equal match in arms for the veteran Trojan.

> Already the Rutulians deemed their man
> O'ermatched in arms, before the fight began.
> First rising fears are whispered through the crowd;
> Then, gathering sound, they murmur more aloud.
> Now, side to side, they measure with their eyes
> The champions' bulk, their sinews, and their size;
> The nearer they approach, the more is known
> The apparent disadvantage of their own.
> DRYDEN, *AEneid*, BOOK XII.

Then Ju-tur'na, the sister of Turnus, knowing of the feeling among the Rutulians, resolved to bring about a violation of the truce which had been made. The goddess Juno had instigated her to do so, telling her that the combat with AEneas would be fatal to her brother, and urging her to prevent it. With this object Juturna, who, being a favorite of Jupiter, had been by him made a sea-nymph, and immortal, went into the midst of the Rutulians, and assuming the form of Ca'mers, an illustrious warrior of their nation, thus addressed them. "Is it not a shame, Rutulians, to permit one man to expose his life to danger for you all? We are greater in number than the enemy and equal in valor. If Turnus die in this fight, he indeed shall be famous forever, but we who sit here inactive, shall, after losing our country, be the slaves of haughty masters."

These words incited the Rutulians to a desire for war, but Juturna still further inflamed their minds by a singular omen. She caused to appear before them in the sky an eagle pursuing a flock of swans. The eagle swooped down upon the swans where they had alighted on the water of the river, and seizing one in its talons, was carrying it off. But suddenly the flock of swans arose, and darting in a solid body upon the eagle, attacked him with such force that he dropped his prey and flew off into the clouds.

The Rutulians understood the meaning of this spectacle, and with loud shouts they began to make preparations for battle. One of their number, the augur To-lum'ni-us, cried out to them to take up their swords and fall upon the Trojan foreigner after the example of the birds who, by united action, had just vanquished their enemy. Then rushing forward, Tolumnius cast a spear into the ranks of the Trojans. Whizzing through the air it struck an Arcadian youth, one of nine brothers who were standing together in the Etrurian lines, and penetrating his side stretched him dead on the field.

Thus the truce was broken, and immediately a fierce battle began, warriors on both sides hurling their darts and plying their swords, the very altars being overthrown in the struggle. Latinus in deep grief and disappointment retired from the scene, now that all hope of peace was at an end. But the Trojan chief, with his head uncovered, stretched forth his unarmed hand, and earnestly appealed to his own people. "Whither do you rush?" he cried. "How has this discord arisen? Restrain your rage, for the league is now formed, and all its terms settled." While thus endeavoring to restore peace, the pious AEneas himself was severely wounded.

 —While he spoke, unmindful of defence,
A winged arrow struck the pious prince.
But whether from some human hand it came,
Or hostile god, is left unknown by fame;
No human hand, or hostile god, was found,
To boast the triumph of so base a wound.
  DRYDEN, *AEneid*, BOOK XII.

AEneas was led away to his tent, bleeding from his wound. Then Turnus called for his war chariot and his arms, and drove furiously over the plain into the midst of the Trojans, dealing death around him on every side.

> He drives impetuous, and, where'er he goes,
> He leaves behind a lane of slaughtered foes.
>   DRYDEN, *AEneid*, BOOK XII.

One brave Trojan warrior named Phe'geus made a gallant fight against Turnus. Leaping in front of the chariot, and seizing the bridles, he strove with all his might to bring the horses to a stand. While he was being dragged along, clinging to the pole, a thrust from the lance of Turnus pierced his coat of mail and inflicted a slight wound. Still the heroic Phegeus held on, and, turning towards his foe, endeavored to reach him with his sword, but just then, coming against the chariot wheels, he was hurled to the ground, and in a moment Turnus, with one blow, struck off his head.

Meanwhile, AEneas attended by Mnestheus, the faithful Achates, and the young Iulus, lay bleeding in his camp. The barb of the arrow by which he had been wounded still remained fixed in the flesh, and not even the skillful surgeon I-a'pis, whom Apollo himself had instructed in medicine, could extract it. But the goddess Venus once more came to the relief of her son. While Iapis was fomenting the wound with water, the goddess, unseen, dipped into the vessel a branch of dit'ta-ny, a plant famous for its healing qualities. At the same time she injected celestial ambrosia, and juice of the all-curing herb pan-a-ce'a.

Instantly the arrow dropped out, the wound healed up, and the Trojan chief recovered his full strength and vigor. Then Iapis exclaimed, "Not by human hand has this cure been effected. Some powerful god, AEneas, has saved you for great enterprises." Immediately the hero put on his armor; and before going out into the battle-field, he tenderly embraced his son and spoke to him words of counsel and encouragement.

> In his mailed arms his child he pressed,
> Kissed through his helm, and thus addressed:
> "Learn of your father to be great,
> Of others to be fortunate.
> This hand awhile shall be your shield
> And lead you safe from field to field;
> When grown yourself to manhood's prime,
> Remember those of former time,
> Recall each venerable name,
>   And catch heroic fire
> From Hector's and AEneas' fame,

Your uncle and your sire."
CONINGTON, *AEneid*, BOOK XII.

AEneas now went forth to the fight. The chiefs and their followers, encouraged by the appearance of their leader, slew numbers of the enemy, including the augur Tolumnius, who had first broken the truce. But the Trojan hero himself sought only for Turnus, and he pursued him over the plain. Juturna seeing this, assumed the shape and likeness of Me-tis'cus, her brother's charioteer, and taking his place upon the chariot, drove rapidly through the field, now here now there, but ever keeping at a distance from the pursuing Trojan chief.

> She steers a various course among the foes;
> Now here, now there, her conquering brother shows;
> Now with a straight, now with a wheeling flight,
> She turns and bends, but shuns the single fight.
> AEneas, fired with fury, breaks the crowd,
> And seeks his foe, and calls by name aloud;
> He runs within a narrower ring, and tries
> To stop the chariot, but the chariot flies.
> DRYDEN, *AEneid*, BOOK XII.

At length AEneas resolved to bring the battle and the war to a speedy end. While pursuing Turnus, he had noticed that the city was left without defence, all the Latian and Rutulian troops being engaged in the field. Calling his chiefs quickly together, he told them of his plan. "The city before us," said he, "is the center of the enemy's strength. It is now in our power. This day we may overturn it, and lay its smoking towers level with the ground. Am I to wait until it pleases Turnus to accept my challenge? Quickly bring firebrands, and very soon we shall establish peace."

The Trojan forces were at once marshalled, and led in a solid battalion to the walls, where a vigorous assault forthwith commenced. Some rushed to the gates and slew the first they met, others hurled darts into the city, and others, by means of scaling ladders, sought to climb over the ramparts. AEneas in a loud voice called the gods to witness that he was now for the second time compelled to fight, and that for a second time a solemn league had been violated by the Latians. Within the town dissension broke out among the alarmed citizens, some urging that the gates should be opened to the Trojans, others taking up arms to defend the walls.

Turnus was in a distant part of the field when he heard of the attack on the city. A messenger rode up to him in haste with the intelligence that AEneas was about to overthrow the stately towers of Latium, and that already flaming torches had been applied to the roofs. Then Turnus saw that the moment for action had come, and he cried out to his sister (for notwithstanding her disguise he had known her from the first): "Now, now, sister, my destiny prevails. Forbear to further stop me. Let me follow whither the gods call. I am resolved to enter the lists with AEneas. No longer shall you see me in disgrace. Whatever bitterness there is in death I am ready to endure it."

So saying, Turnus sprang from his chariot, and bounding over the plain, rushed into the midst of the combatants at the gates of the city. With outstretched arms he made a sign to his friends, and called upon them in a loud voice: "Rutulians and Latians, cease fighting. Whatever fortune of the war remains is mine. It is for me alone by my sword to put an end to this strife."

AEneas, hearing the challenge of Turnus, forsook the lofty walls and towers, and hastened to encounter his foe. The hosts on both sides laid down their arms. A space was cleared on the open plain, and immediately the two heroes rushed to the combat, with hurling of darts and clashing of swords and shields.

> They launch their spears; then hand to hand they meet;
> The trembling soil resounds beneath their feet;
> Their bucklers clash; thick blows descend from high,
> And flakes of fire from their hard helmets fly.
>   DRYDEN, *AEneid*, BOOK XII.

The great fight now began. Turnus aimed a mighty blow at AEneas, raising himself on tiptoes, and adding to the force of the stroke the whole weight of his body. But the blade snapped in two as it struck the armor of the Trojan hero, thus leaving the Rutulian chief at the mercy of his foe. The weapon was one he had hastily snatched up instead of his own when mounting his chariot for the first fight of the day. It had served his purpose so long as he used it only on fleeing Trojans, but when it came against the armor made by Vulcan it broke like ice. The unfortunate Rutulian now turned and fled over the field, calling loudly on his friends to bring him his sword. AEneas followed in pursuit, threatening death to any one who should venture to approach, and thus five times round the lists they ran.

> Five times they circle round the place,
> Five times the winding course retrace;
> No trivial game is here; the strife
> Is waged for Turnus' own dear life.
>   CONINGTON, *AEneid*, BOOK XII.

Finding that he could not overtake the fleeing Turnus, AEneas resolved again to make trial of his celestial spear. At the outset of the combat he had hurled this weapon with such force, that it fixed itself deep in the stump of a wild olive tree that stood in the field. The tree had been sacred to the deity Faunus, but the Trojans had cut it down to make a clear ground for their military movements. When AEneas attempted to wrench the spear out, Turnus prayed to Faunus to detain the weapon.

> "O Faunus! pity! and thou, mother Earth,
> Where I thy foster-son received my birth,
> Hold fast the steel! If my religious hand
> Your plant has honored, which your foes profaned,
> Propitious hear my pious prayer."
> DRYDEN, *AEneid*, BOOK XII.

But now the power of the gods was exercised on behalf of both heroes. While AEneas struggled in vain to extricate the javelin, Juturna, again taking the form of Metiscus, ran forward to her brother and gave him his own sword. Then Venus came to the aid of her son, and the steel was easily drawn from the tough root. Once more the two chiefs stood ready for the combat, the one relying on his trusty sword, the other, on the spear which a god had made.

Meanwhile the goddess Juno, sitting in a yellow cloud, was watching the combat, and Jupiter, coming near, advised her to abandon her hopeless enmity to the Trojans, and forbade her to further resist the decree of heaven. Juno was now ready to yield, but on one condition— "When by this marriage they establish peace, let the people of Latium retain their ancient name and language. Let Latium subsist. Let the sons of Rome rise to imperial power by means of Italian valor. Troy has perished. Let the name also perish." To this the king of heaven replied: "I grant what you desire. The Italians shall retain their native language and customs. The Trojans shall settle in Latium and mingle with its people and all shall be called Latins and have but one speech."

> "All shall be Latium; Troy without a name;
> And her lost sons forget from whence they came.
> From blood so mixed a pious race shall flow,
> Equal to gods, excelling all below.
> No nation more respect to you shall pay,
> Or greater offerings on your altars lay."
> Juno consents, well pleased that her desires
> Had found success, and from the cloud retires.
> DRYDEN, *AEneid*, BOOK XII.

Then Jupiter sent one of the Furies down to the field of battle, in the form of an owl, and the evil bird flew backwards and forwards in the sight of Turnus, flapping its wings. The chief, knowing that this was an unfavorable omen, hesitated to advance, and AEneas calling to him aloud cried,

"Turnus, why do you further decline to fight? It is not in running that we must now try our skill, but with arms in close conflict." "I have no fear of you, insulting foe," answered Turnus. "My dread is of the gods, who are against me." As he spoke, he saw on the ground before him a huge stone, such as only a man of giant strength could lift. Seizing it and poising it over his head he rushed forward, and hurled it against the enemy.

> But wildering fears his mind unman;
> Running, he knew not that he ran,
>   Nor throwing that he threw;
> Heavily move his sinking knees;
> The streams of life wax dull and freeze;
> The stone, as through the void it passed,
> Reached not the measure of its cast,
>   Nor held its purpose true.
>   CONINGTON; *AEneid*, BOOK XII.

AEneas, now taking careful aim, and putting forth the whole strength of his body, hurled his fatal spear. Like a whirlwind it flew, and with mighty force breaking through the shield and corselet of the Rutulian chief, pierced his thigh. Down to the earth he sank on his knees, and the Trojan chief rushed forward sword in hand. Then the vanquished hero besought the conqueror: "I have deserved my fate, and I do not deprecate it, yet if any regard for an unhappy father can move you, have compassion on the aged Daunus. You too had such a father. You have triumphed. Lavinia is yours. Persist not further in hate."

AEneas was much affected by this appeal. It almost moved him to spare the life of his foe, but the belt of Pallas which the wounded man wore sealed his fate. As soon as it caught the eye of the Trojan he raised his sword and with one blow avenged the death of the brave son of Evander.

> Then, roused anew to wrath, he loudly cries
> (Flames, while he spoke, came flashing from his eyes),
> "Traitor! dost thou, dost thou to grace pretend,
> Clad, as thou art, in trophies of my friend?
> To his sad soul a grateful offering go!
> 'Tis Pallas, Pallas gives this deadly blow!"
> He raised his arm aloft, and at the word,
> Deep in his bosom drove the shining sword.
> The streaming blood distained his arms around;
> And the disdainful soul came rushing through the wound.
>   DRYDEN, *AEneid*, BOOK XII.

Here ends the story of AEneas as related by Vergil. There was no more to be told, that could properly come within the limits of the subject, as set forth in the opening lines of the AEneid:

> Arms and the man I sing, who, forced by Fate,
> And haughty Juno's unrelenting hate,
> Expelled and exiled, left the Trojan shore.
> Long labors, both by sea and land, he bore,
> And in the doubtful war, before he won
> The Latian realm, and built the destined town.

The poet undertook to tell about the wanderings of the hero, and his long labors both by sea and land, up to the time he won a settlement in Italy. This was accomplished by the death of Turnus, which put an end to the war. The brave Rutulian chief made a gallant fight, but the fates were against him. He would probably have been the victor had his antagonist been any other than the man of destiny, who had the decrees of heaven always on his side.

As to the subsequent history of AEneas, the Roman traditions tell us that he married the princess Lavinia, and built a city which was called after her name—Lavinium. Upon the death of his father-in-law, Latinus, he became king of Latium. But though he was then in possession of his long promised settlement, his wars were not entirely over, for we are told that he fought a battle with the Rutulians who, though their king was dead, were still unwilling to submit to a foreigner. In this battle, which took place on the bank of the river Numicus, the Trojan hero mysteriously disappeared and was seen no more. Some say he was drowned in the river, and that the Latins, not finding the body, supposed he had been taken up to heaven, and therefore offered him sacrifices as a god.

On the death of the hero, his son Iulus succeeded him, and built the city of Alba Longa, which was ruled for many centuries by kings of the line of AEneas, whose descendants were the founders of Rome.

> From whence the race of Alban Fathers come,
> And the long glories of majestic Rome.

Milton Keynes UK
Ingram Content Group UK Ltd.
UKHW031146311024
450535UK00004B/131